W9-AAP-687

PENGUIN CRIME FICTION

BACKTRACK

Joseph Hansen's verse has appeared in *The New Yorker*, *The Atlantic*, and *Harper's*; his short stories in magazines as various as *South Dakota Review* and *Mystery Monthly*. In the 1960s he published eight novels under the pen name James Colton. In the 1970s Joseph Hansen launched the celebrated Dave Brandstetter mystery series, which now includes six titles: *Death Claims*, *Fadeout*, *Gravedigger*, *The Man Everybody Was Afraid Of*, *Skinflick*, and *Troublemaker*. His much praised mainstream novel, *A Smile in His Lifetime* (1981), was written on a grant from the National Endowment for the Arts. Mr. Hansen lives, teaches, and writes in Los Angeles.

Backtrack

JOSEPH HANSEN

Penguin Books

Penguin Books Ltd, Harmondsworth,
Middlesex, England
Penguin Books, 40 West 23rd Street,
New York, New York 10010, U.S.A.
Penguin Books Australia Ltd, Ringwood,
Victoria, Australia
Penguin Books Canada Limited, 2801 John Street,
Markham, Ontario, Canada L3R 1B4
Penguin Books (N.Z.) Ltd, 182–190 Wairau Road,
Auckland 10, New Zealand

First published in the United States of America by
The Countryman Press 1982
Published in Penguin Books 1983

LIBRARY OF CONGRESS CATALOGING IN PUBLICATION DATA
Hansen, Joseph, 1923–
  Backtrack.
  I. Title.
PS3558.A513B3 1983   813'.54   83-4128
ISBN 0 14 00.6782 5

Printed in the United States of America by
Offset Paperback Mfrs., Inc., Dallas, Pennsylvania
Set in Baskerville

The ground cried my name
Goodbye for being wrong
Love helps the sun
But not enough . . .

          —Theodore Roethke

backtrack

now the room is big, with yellow rainstains on the ceiling, like maps of nowhere. Heavy surf shakes the house sometimes, and paint flakes off the ceiling and snows on me. The house is tall old frame. It faces a beach with dune-fences and a lonely steel and concrete fishing pier. I can see these in the mirror my savior and protector, Catch, has taken off a thriftshop dresser and rigged high on the wall, tilted to face the window. I can also see myself, legs in plaster casts, chest and shoulder bandaged, five feet four, one hundred ten pounds, almost eighteen but looking thirteen—in a funky bed with magazines, pizza tins, paperbacks, and Colonel Sanders buckets.

But that I'm used to. What I'm not used to are flowers. And this morning, flowers crowd the room—chrysanthemums, white, yellow, dark gold, on the floor, the dresser, banked up the walls. Can it be that I am laid out for burial? No. I can move. I lift my head, blinking. It's cold. The mirror shows me fog outside, so thick I can't see the end of the pier. The room door is open. Coffee smells and the noise of hard rock radio comes up the staircase. The air is edgy with the smell of chrysanthemums, like a florist's icebox. When Catch comes in, black and beautiful, wearing a Navy surplus turtleneck and Navy surplus dungarees, I say to him:

"Somebody died before they could take delivery?"

"Naw, baby." Catch sets the mugs down under the bedside lamp that is a brown figure of Kwan Yin, the Chinese goddess of mercy, which Catch claims he found in a Beverly Hills trash barrel. The coffee steam trickles up past her face, that has a faint smile on it. Catch bends and kisses me. His mouth is cold with the cold of the house. Past his tight little black ear, I watch Kwan Yin smile. "Naw, baby—somebody got well and checked out."

"Somebody with that many flowers was very sick."

"Famous." Catch picks up the pillows I pushed onto the floor last night. He lifts me and stacks the pillows behind me against the wall and sets me up. I can do it, but I let Catch do it because he likes to. I shiver, and Catch finds me a sweatshirt and puts me into it, managing me as if I were a doll. "Hannah Brown, suffering from exhaustion."

"In the L.A. County General Hospital?"

"To avoid publicity. With two maids, and a big male secretary that put the make on me in a broom closet." Catch keeps a very straight face. "I said, 'Sir, I am bespoken. I am to be a bride tomorrow morning. Please!' But all the time he's crowding me into the corner, breathing hot lust all over me. Hands everywhere. What a secretary! He must can use four typewriters at once. 'Please,' I begged piteously, while he tore my fragile garments and forced me brutally to my knees among the mops. Whoo-ee!" Catch rolls his eyes, 1930's movie nigger style. He nearly cracks up laughing, but not quite. " 'Please,' I implored, 'what will my husband-to-be, the Senator from Alabama—what will he say?' "

I laugh. "I can see you resisting."

"I did." Catch's eyes grow round with sincerity. "I silently struggled in that suffocating darkness. I clawed, I kicked. A young Southron lady's virtue is all she has." He lays a hand on his chest and bats his eyelashes.

"Hannah Brown," I say, "is doing a show in New York."

"She jetted here. For anonymity. Complete rest."

I try the coffee. "What was she exhausted from?"

"All that heavy jewelry. She's just too frail."

"How did you get out of the broom closet?" I ask.

"I didn't." Catch shuts his eyes, hangs his head, drops his voice. "Not before he had his way with me. Oh!" This is a wail. He turns his back, hunches his shoulders, covers his face with his hands. "I am so humiliated. But what could I do? I am a delicate creature, gently nurtured, as easily crushed as a honeysuckle blossom." He faces me, chewing his lower lip, clutching the turtleneck at his throat. "When it happened, I wanted to die. I snatched up a bottle of Lysol, but he dashed it from my lips. Oh, please. . . !" Catch falls to his knees by the bed, grabs my hands, looks up at me with tears in his eyes. "Dear husband, don't condemn me, Senator, honey. I did all a weak woman could do. Don't send me away to bear my baby in shame and sorrow."

"You want to take me to the bathroom, now?" I ask.

Catch sighs and gets up. "You never believe me."

3

I grin. "I can't wait to see that baby."

Catch laughs and throws the covers back and picks me up. As if I were made of styrofoam. Catch is thin. I don't know where he keeps all the muscle, but it's there. When Catch sets me on the john and starts to leave so I can empty myself in private, I say:

"But those flowers didn't get there till whoever it was was a corpse—right?"

Catch turns, with the doorknob in his hand. "I brought them because I love you. If you don't like the vibrations, I can throw them out."

"Don't throw them out," I say.

It isn't much, but it's enough. Catch smiles as if I had given him flowers. He shuts the door.

His shift at the hospital these days is from midnight to eight in the morning. It's miles from here, and his Volkswagen is old—brown with rust on the outside, brown with dried blood, mine, on the inside—so he never wakes me till about a quarter to nine. Like this morning, he tips hot coffee into me to get my bowels working, then totes me to the bathroom. Totes is his word.

After that, he feeds me. For years, I didn't know there was anything for breakfast but Sugar Pops. These days, I get eggs turned over easy in deep butter, slabs of juicy ham, fried mush, porkchops, buckwheat cakes, country sausage, hashbrown potatoes. What I got yesterday was cornbread fresh out of the oven with melted butter and molasses. "You'd think you wanted to marry me," I said, and Catch said, "You'd be right."

Next he bathes me. I could do it for myself, now,

but at first I couldn't. And I haven't had the heart to stop Catch. How I feel is, Christ, if somebody wants to touch you naked, somebody who's saved your life, for God sake, who keeps you alive—you let them. Then Catch sacks out till about four and I read. There is a monster television set, but once it's turned on, there's no way I can turn it off— Catch didn't know where they kept the remote control switches in the store-room of the shop he ripped the TV set off from. Anyway, I like reading better than TV. I think of my mind as if it were an animal trapped under a bowl in the dark that has to be fed or maybe drugged to keep it from killing itself. With television on, after a while my mind starts making up crazy songs and singing them loudly and not paying attention.

After Catch gets up and splashes around in the bathroom, we have drinks. Catch's are ladylike— Daiquiris, Margaritas, Silver Fizzes. I am into Bourbon. It reminds me of the smell of the dark, padded leather places Babe used to work, and I like remembering Babe. She's about all I do like remembering now. Then Catch rattles off in his car for take-out dim sum or burritos or burgers and fries, and we eat supper. Nights, we play gin or double solitaire, Catch sitting cross-legged on the bed with me, cards laid out on the blanket over my casts, the radio tuned to the top forty hits, and Catch's shoulders moving, and now and then his fingers snapping, to the beat. Oh, if I've been reading something exciting in *Scientific American* or *Newsweek* or *Psychology Today*, I may talk to Catch about it. He looks alert, nods and shakes his head, and says things like *Yeah?* and *No shit?* and *Out of sight, man.* But I can see he's really only being polite, and pretty soon his eyes glaze, and I give up.

On his day off, he gets up early and goes out and does the wash at the coin laundry and shops—or shoplifts. He is always bringing me expensive gifts. Like the Kwan Yin lamp, which is ironic because of my homicidal future plans that Catch knows nothing about. Or the radio. Or an electric razor when I hardly shave at all, being too young and too blond. His last present to me was a wristwatch that bristles with fancy stops—so I can see the seconds dragging into hours, into days, and, maybe, finally, into enough weeks so I can get out of these miserable casts.

Unless Catch gets busted. He's smart, and he moves quickly and quietly—like when he got me out of that nightmare hospital—but he's outnumbered, like anybody black in this country, and, worse than that, he's too kind. It makes me nervous. Catch rips off pills from the hospital and gives them to crazies—not sells, gives. All somebody has to do is whine to him, cry a little, freak out, and Catch saves them with whatever they want. Black Jesus on the beach. Only sometime one of the ones he performs his miracles for is going to babble to The Man where they got what sent them up or down or into space—and that will finish Catch. Or a paunchy rental cop in the local discount supermarket will hit on him when he has an economy half-gallon of whisky under his poncho. I hope it never happens, but mainly I hope it doesn't happen soon. I'll lie up here and starve to death in my own mess.

Catch swears he never takes chances. If he can't steal something easy, he pays for it. But I know he can't pay for much. Orderlies hardly make enough to keep themselves alive, let alone someone extra. Like, he doesn't rent this place. It belongs to Doc Gallo's crazy old mother who is up in Camarillo State Mental Hospital, dying of memories. Doc hardly comes near this house, hates it. It was just standing here, collapsing. So Catch got it free. I know that if nothing happens to Catch, he won't desert me, never. He doesn't even know my name, but I am it. He lives for me. He'd die for me. Which makes me sad and ashamed.

Now Catch is walking out of the room, carrying the red molded plastic pan of soapy water from my wash, when somebody rattles the downstairs door. Catch almost drops the pan. He sets it on the dresser and, in the hall, squats to look through the broken bannisters. The door at the foot of the staircase has a big oval of glass in it. I have only seen it once—the night when Catch brought me here, along the hall from the back of the house, which is the way Catch always comes and goes—through the kitchen. I was nearly dead from loss of blood and from the painkillers they gave me after they set my broken legs, but I remember that glass in the front door. It is white with sea salt, like a cataract on a giant eye. I don't know how Catch expects to see through it now. But evidently he can. Maybe daylight makes the difference.

"It's Dame Myra Hiss," he says.

So. It isn't Sage come to kill me, and my heart quits being a fist in my throat, and I listen with a grin as Catch skitters down the stairs, opens the door, and the giddy birdcries start. Dame Myra Hiss is a male nurse named Howard Williams. That hospital swarms with faggots. I hear this one ask:

"How's your mother?"

And I have to laugh, because that's me. Catch tells whoever comes to the house that his old mother is up here very sick. Terminal. It's a good cover. Who'd want to look at some rotting old lady? And when he has parties, he locks the door to my room, so no one stoned or juiced can stumble in by mistake. But he doesn't neglect me. He checks me out pretty often. And I don't miss much, because the sound comes up through the floor, laughter, shrieks of travestied female outrage, booming reggae or rock or disco. There's almost always pot, and he smuggles that in to me too, and I lie quietly blowing my mind and spinning the radio dial trying to find Bach. I like Bach because it doesn't remind me of anything.

And I don't need to be reminded. . . .

then Babe was asleep and I was pouring milk over a bowlful of Sugar Pops when I noticed the folded copy of *Daily Variety* on the kitchen counter. One paragraph had a lipstick circle around it. It was headed THESP DIES. Actor Eric Tarr, it said, was found dead outside the building where he lived in Hollywood. His neck was broken and his skull fractured. He had apparently jumped or fallen from the window of his fourth floor canyon apartment. His latest film, still unreleased, was—

I stopped reading because I'd slopped milk on the Formica. I got a yellow square of cellulose sponge and wiped it up. I put the milk carton away, found a spoon, sat down. I ate, but I didn't taste. I felt numb. Eric Tarr was my father. I'd never met him, never seen him, except on television in old movies, and now and then in episodes of cop shows. He looked like me—small, and fair haired, and on the pretty side of handsome.

Babe never said much about him except *That son of a bitch*. But she didn't make me change channels when he was on the box or, like the books say, try to turn me against him. She didn't miss him. She had more men around than she could use. What she talked about when she talked about Eric was how he walked out on her when I was six months old. It was really all I knew. But I couldn't ask her to tell me more now. She was asleep.

She'd be asleep till noon. She played piano in bars. This kept her out late. Babe was good at what she did, but she never kept gigs long, mostly on account of men. Oh, once, when I was seven, eight, nine—she played one place, The Cove, in Oxnard, for three years. We even lived in a house. She'd married the bar owner, a nice fat guy named Cliff Stein. But it didn't last, and she never got another gig like it. She and I kept moving. We lived in a trailer. A kid switches schools a lot, that way. I never had time to make friends before we were on our way to another town.

When I got home from school, Luther Schlag, six feet three, two hundred fifty pounds of local law-enforcement, was standing under the tin awning beside the trailer, drinking Coors from a tall can. He nodded and tightened his mouth in what he thought was a smile. He and I are from different planets and we both know it. Inside the trailer, Babe was steamy and perfumy from a shower, and sitting there in her bra and pantyhose, putting on her face to take to the Casa Camino. Luther would drive her there in his pickup with the giant tires and the rifle racked up in the cab, have dinner with her sometime, drive her home. I said:

"Will Eric be all right? Will somebody bury him?"

"He's had his own life for ages and ages," she said, "and I've had mine. I can't worry about him now. If he doesn't have anybody to bury him, that's his problem."

"I was going to ask you to tell me about him."

"You wouldn't enjoy it," she said. "Anyway, Luther's waiting."

"I'd like to go to the funeral," I said.

Babe had a brush in her hand for smoothing makeup. The hairs of it were kind of orange color. She laid it down and looked at me in the powder-dusty glass of the special, light-bulb-framed mirror she'd set up on the little built-in dressing-table. One of her eyes had its false lashes on, and the other didn't. The one without them looked naked. She blinked, and the sparkly stuff on the fake lashes twinkled. That eye seemed friendly. The other one looked cold and surprised.

"What? What in the world for?"

"You don't kill yourself if anybody cares about you," I said. "He was my father. I better go."

She shrugged and picked up another eyelash

from the table that was strewn with Q-Tips, nail-polish bottles, wads of Kleenex. She dabbed glue on the lash, leaned toward the mirror as if she were going to kiss herself, shut the naked eye in what looked like a slow, drunken wink, and stuck the thing into place. She blinked and carefully finger-tipped away a tear.

"Suit yourself," she said. "How are you going to get there?"

"It won't cost much by Greyhound," I said.

"It will cost more than it's worth." She stood and pulled a green dress over her head, and I helped her smooth it down, and I zipped it up the back for her.

"I can hitch-hike," I said.

She put on beads and bracelets. "Suit yourself," she said again, and leaned to the mirror to fit on her wig. It made her a redhead, and matched her lipstick and nailpolish. She looked beautiful. She said, "I don't understand you, with your brains, being sentimental about a man you've never even met."

My brains were always a marvel to Babe. She mentioned them almost every time we talked. She admired my brains the way I admired her looks. I am a freak. My scores go off the top of the IQ tests. They get thrown out because they wreck the norm curves. Sometimes the no-chin hick teachers who administer the tests tell Babe I'm a genius. But you have to be a genius *at* something and there is no something I know about that I want to be a genius at.

"I don't understand it either," I said. "But I want to go."

"So go," she said. "I think it's sweet." She could say things like that and mean them.

We both heard Luther Schlag crumple the empty beer can in his fist outside.

"I'll see you when I get back," I said.

Babe kissed my forehead. "Bye," she said, and went.

That was how she was. She always left me on my own. It wouldn't have worked well with most kids. But if all you really care about is reading, you don't get into a whole hell of a lot of trouble. Because I'd pestered her, Babe had taught me to read herself, when I was two and a half, using old copies of *Current Smash Hits* and *The Enquirer*. Reaching my teens didn't change me. I never ached to play football the way most jockey-size kids do. I didn't yearn to ride surfboards or steal cars. Athletics made me yawn. When the highschool coach made me run around the track, I read books while I ran. So Babe had no reason to worry about me. Maybe she was selfish and irresponsible and wouldn't have worried about me if I'd been a werewolf, but I wasn't, and she didn't, and that was great.

But she never gave me money. This didn't matter if we were in a town with a public library, but it did if I had to buy my own books off the paperback rack at the supermarket on the highway. Then I had to scrounge for bread. Not bread literally. Babe fed me well—mostly with take-outs from the restaurants where she played. And she bought me new clothes a lot, because buying new ones was less trouble than laundering the old ones. She wasn't domestic. But if I wanted books—it didn't matter how awed she was by my brains—I had to buy them myself.

I started pretty early, writing other kids' papers in school, drawing their maps, doing their arithmetic homework. Lately the money was better because I was doing it for clods at the local two-year college. Still, as I counted it my private hoard that afternoon was fourteen grubby dollar bills. It was two hundred fifty miles to L.A. I stuffed the bills into a pocket of my white Levi's, dragged down from an overhead storage compartment a dimestore suitcase, dusted the spilled facepowder out of it, and folded into it my suit and black shoes, a shirt, tie, shorts, t-shirts and socks. I'd had a shower at school. I guessed I was ready. I shrugged into my new red windbreaker jacket, pushed the paperback of *The Mind of the Dolphin* into a hip pocket, and locked the trailer after me.

I got rides, but none of them took me more than twenty miles at a hitch, so that by two thirty in the morning I had only reached Goleta. Sitting shivering on the suitcase at the side of the Coast Highway with the ocean breathing cold on my back, I began to think the manufacturers had called in all the cars in California for dangerous defects. L.A. was still a hundred miles off. I looked for the moon. Nowhere. I looked up the highway, and a car was coming.

I stood up, and it slowed down. I sprinted after it and then, when I saw it close up, I didn't know whether I was happy or not. It was an old, beat-up van painted with tangled designs in bright colors—not well-painted, very amateurish, in what looked like kindergarten poster paint. Words were twisted among the vines and flowers. LOVE. DOPE. A side door slid open. Loud rock music came out. I climbed into smoke. So thick it made me cough.

"Shut the door," somebody said.

I shut it, and the van jerked, and I fell onto the seat. There were three people in the front. They all had long hair. I couldn't tell what sex they were. Then the driver turned me a grin, and shouted that his name was Hughie, and that this was Margaret and that was Fran. I shouted back that my name was Alan, and thanks for the ride. No one turned down the radio or tape cartridge, or whatever it was—so conversation wouldn't work.

I sat back and checked who was next to me. He was middle-aged and very fat, with a bushy black beard, steel-rimmed glasses and a derby hat with a flower decal pasted over its dome. He was asleep, slumped down with his hands in the pockets of greasy corduroys, and his feet up on a duffel bag. Beyond him, a frail-looking teen-age girl held a stick of burning incense in her fingers and a cloth bundle in her lap. Her face was pale and framed in long, straight, dark hair. Her nose was thin and beaky, but she had big, shiny black eyes. They were watching me, and she smiled.

"Hi," I yelled. "What's your name?"

"Gus," she screamed. "Gus."

The fat man didn't wake up. He twitched a little and started to snore. His puffy lips inside the beard made soft, exhaust pipe sounds. Gus sat there smiling at me across the dirty plaid flannel mountain of the man's belly while miles of black nothing unrolled past the windows. My face got tired of smiling back at her, and I finally shouted for her to come over to where I was. She slid her window open a crack and poked the incense out. She dug something from her bundle, jammed the bundle into the seat-corner, and climbed over the back of the seat into what looked in the dark, at a guess, like instrument cases and loudspeakers. She crawled over the seat back, the truck lurched, and she fell on me, giggling.

By reflex, I grabbed her. It felt good. I'd never hugged anybody in my life but Babe. This girl was different, very fragile and small and warm. It was probably like holding a child, only she wasn't a child—she was old as me, maybe even older. She gave me a quick little kiss and wedged herself between me and the door. The fat man didn't move. When I nudged him he only grunted. Gus had a little leather pouch and a pack of Zigzag papers. She made a cigarette, lit the ragged end, dragged off the other end, deep and slow, held the smoke, and passed the cigarette to me.

It wasn't any long reach. We were practically glued together. We only fit into the space the fat man left us because we were both so small. I dragged at the cigarette the way she had, only it was raw smoke, and I coughed it out fast at the first try, and my eyes watered. She watched me with her big, glossy eyes, and I tried again, and got a lungful this time, and held onto it a while. I could feel her little breasts nudging my upper arm like soft fists. We smoked the thing down till everything began to seem like a dream. When the cigarette was too short, she slotted it out the window, and snuggled down with her head on my shoulder.

Her breath made little feathers of warmth against the side of my neck. I looked. Her eyes weren't closed. They were watching me like before, and she was smiling like before. So I kissed her smile. She clamped a hand on the back of my neck and held onto the kiss the way she'd held onto the smoke. Her tongue pushed at my teeth. I opened them, and somehow my tongue was in the smoky, soft dark of her mouth. Her hand found the tab of my jacket and zipped it down. She tugged out my T-shirt and ran her hand up under it on my skin. It felt very nice.

She was wearing something shapeless and long. I guess it was made out of cotton and it seemed to be printed with little flowers. She wriggled her small self inside it and mumbled urgently without taking her mouth off mine, and I guessed what she wanted and stretched a hand down as far as I could reach and worked the cloth up along her legs until my fingers found the hem. Hell, she wasn't wearing anything under it. I was startled. Things were moving a little fast for me. I'd never done any of this before. I really hadn't thought too much about it. Not the way some of the boys my age I'd met in different schools seemed to— they never thought about anything else. I wondered if I was undersexed. But I took a breath and moved my hand on up and squeezed her little breasts gently. They felt very soft and tender.

But there was nothing soft and tender about the way her fingers were fighting the brass button at the waist of my Levi's. It startled me. For a second I turned numb. Then I felt sorry for her trying so hard and getting noplace and I worked the button for her. She didn't let me slide the zipper. She did that herself. And her hand seemed to know a lot about jockey shorts. And a tire blew out.

The van slewed and went sideways along the highway for a while, screaming and throwing sparks. Then it rolled over, while everybody shouted and fell on top of everybody else and the junk in the back clanked and thumped, and the radio went on blaring rock. The van hit the beach and stopped on its side, and we crawled out through the top doors. No one was hurt. Everyone was laughing. Mainly at me. I stood there on the four A.M. sand, bare-assed. My pants and shorts had peeled off when the fat man dragged me up out of the van. I didn't care. What had happened, or almost happened, had felt sensational. And I'd found Gus. I just grinned.

Hughie went away in his fuzzy brown natural haircut and cowboy boots, to find a pay phone and get somebody to come pick them up. The fat man and the girls took off their clothes and went into the dark morning surf and laughed and splashed each other and played tag. I climbed up the van and fell inside and dug around in the dark for my pants and shorts and suitcase, threw them out, and climbed out after them, getting a grease smudge from the door-latch on my red jacket. I shook the sand out of my jockeys and put them on. I walked down the dry sand to the wet sand, dragging the Levi's, stepping over their dropped clothing. I stood and watched Gus play, a shadow child. When she noticed me, she stopped and tilted her head. Then she came out of the surf, dripping, shaking back her wet hair.

"Aren't you coming in?"

"I have to get to my father's funeral."

The fat man came up. He was matted all over with mangy-looking hair. When he ran, he bruised the sand and made it shake. He wrapped his arms around Gus from behind and held her, laughing, rocking her a little, nuzzling her hair, while I hated him, and Gus stared at me with big, serious eyes.

"What time is your father's funeral?"

"Eleven." I flapped the Levi's to put them on.

She took my wrist and brought it close to her face to see the dial of my watch, because it still wasn't very light. Her thin little fingers were cold with sea wet but I liked her touching me.

"It's only a little after four," she said. "And it's not all that much farther to L.A., is it? Somebody will come out to get us. Hughie knows a lot of musicians with cars." I didn't know what the fat man did, but now she noticed him and jerked away from him. "Go play with Margaret," she said. "Go play with Fran." He laughed, grabbed her, kissed her, and jogged back into the surf, plowing it up.

"Hughie might run out of dimes." I jerked my Levi's up one leg. "I better try to hitch with someone else." I kicked into the other leg. "Where can I find you later?"

"Do you want to?" She sounded surprised.

I tucked in my T-shirt and zipped my fly. "I love you, Gus," I said.

"Oh-oh," she said.

"Just tell me the address," I said. "I have this freak memory. I won't forget."

"Stay now," she said, and took my hand. Down the beach were dunes and clumps of tall grass. She led me there.

It was hours before one of Hughie's friends came in another battered van to pick us up off the beach. To save time, I changed into my suit and tie while we rattled down the coast to L.A. And the time they were making wasn't bad until they swung off the Coast Road at Santa Monica and hit traffic. Getting to Hollywood was a drag. And it was twenty past eleven when I jumped out and Gus and the rest yelled goodbye at me and the van ground its gears away into the sunbaked smog.

Inside the fake adobe mission that was the funeral chapel, under artfully charred beams, among plastic flowers, muted organ music, stained glass, and leaky sinuses, the wrong cadaver was being told by a bored minister in a this-is-a-recording voice, *I am the resurrection and the life,* and lying there stiff in bronze and pale blue tufted satin, and not believing it.

An usher stood by the carved doors—pinstripe pants, grey silk foulard, shiny rimless glasses. Mint mouthwash blew at me while the usher whispered that my father's funeral was over. The procession would be at the cemetery now. In a dim little room full of dank ferns and caged canaries, I phoned for a taxi. A new funeral every half hour! I didn't let the canaries out, but I thought of it.

By the time I found my father's grave, a pair of Mexicans in starchy brown work clothes was covering it with squares of sod so green they looked dyed. I climbed a slope between new little trees in bandages and splints. Bronze plaques lay in the hungry grass. I set my suitcase down by some discarded flowers and felt futile and guilty. It wasn't my fault I hadn't made it on time. It was just bad luck. And anyway, Eric wouldn't know it. I still felt like crying.

Then I saw the bald man again. He'd been opening a new Bentley when I was paying off the taxi at the foot of the hill. The bald man had half bent to drop onto the genuine cowhide seat. One foot was inside the car, one hand on the steering-wheel. It was an awkward position to pause in, but he'd paused, dead still, staring at me with his mouth half open. I hadn't paid attention. I paid attention now. The man stood on the other side of the grave, wearing a beautiful suit. Dark glasses made it hard to be sure, but the lift of his chin and his stillness made me think he was staring again.

"My God," he said, "it's not possible."

The Mexicans on their knees looked up. "Senor?"

He shook his head at them and stepped around the grave for a closer look at me. Not really close. He kept a yard between us, like a man who's always told himself he isn't afraid of ghosts. He took off the dark glasses. He'd been crying. He shook his head again, and a corner of his mouth smiled.

"No," he said. "Eric was never so young."

"He was my father," I said.

"Unmistakably. That would make you—Alan?"

I nodded, and the bald man held out a hand. It

was long and bony, and the grip was strong. It was also gritty. Was he the one who'd tossed the first handful of dirt into the grave?

"I'm Glen Thornton," he said.

The Mexicans laid the wilting flowers on the new sods and went away with an empty wheelbarrow, green metal, with a thick rubber tire. Thornton watched them with bleak, pale blue eyes.

I asked, "Are you the only one who came?"

"No. Day players thrive on funerals." Thornton crouched and pushed at a brown seam between sods, trying to close it, to make it green. "They gloat. One less among the competition. Improved odds on working next week."

"Didn't he have any friends?"

Thornton stood up quickly. "Ah, don't pay any attention to my bitching. Of course he had friends."

"You don't have to stroke me," I said. "I'm older than I look."

"But still sentimental about friends." Thornton brushed the grave dirt off his hands.

I didn't think I was sentimental about friends. I'd never really had any. "Maybe about my father. That's what my mother claims."

"Babe." Thornton gave the new sods a sad smile. "How is Babe?"

"Beautiful," I said. "Do you know her?"

"She worked for me once. Why does she call you sentimental? Did you write to Eric? Did you see him?"

"Never," I said.

"But you came to his funeral." Thornton hooked the wire loops of the dark glasses over his ears. I saw myself reflected in the lenses. Thornton said, "She's right."

I shrugged. "I'd like to know about him. Can you tell me about him?"

"He could have. Why did you wait till he was dead?"

"It was the first thing he did to attract my attention," I said. "The movies weren't that good."

"And your mother said he was a faggot, and to stay away from him—right?"

"She said he was a son of a bitch," I said. "Was he a faggot?"

"Would I be likely to tell you?"

"You already did, didn't you?"

"And you want to hear more," Thornton said, "from me?"

"You didn't hate him," I said. "You stayed here while they filled the grave. You cried. I'd believe what you told me."

"Find someone else." He walked away.

"Wait." I picked up the suitcase and jogged after him. "Just let me hitch a ride with you. To someplace where I can eat." All I'd had was a wedge of pizza in Lompoc, and a few sunflower seeds from a dime cellophane pack Gus had dug out of her bundle. I told the bald man, "You don't have to talk to me if you don't want to."

He didn't talk. He tooled the Bentley down out of the hills and onto a long white curve of freeway with mountains lost in brown murk to the right. A blue hole was overhead, where it looked as if you could breathe if you could get up there. I said:

"Why I mentioned friends was because he must

have been lonely. You don't commit suicide when people care about you."

"Actors," Thornton said, "don't commit suicide when they have a film about to be released. They want to see their performance. They want to read the reviews. It was quite a big part for Eric, best he'd had in years. He'd made money from it. He wasn't worried about money, for a change. He had a new lover. No—he didn't commit suicide."

"Did he fall?" I asked. "Was he a drunk?"

"He wasn't a drunk," Thornton said.

He slanted the Bentley down an offramp and we wheeled south for a while on a broad street between decorator showrooms and art galleries. Then there began to be only restaurants. I knew a couple of the names but I didn't know the name of the one whose parkinglot we drove into. It was stone, with a deep-eaved shake roof, thick beams, stained glass, and landscaping that looked as if it got replaced every morning.

It was lunchtime. The lot was full of polished Porsches and waxed Aston-Martins. Under an ivy-draped portecochere, a tall kid in forest green uniform with loops of gold braid at one shoulder, and whose face said he'd come to Hollywood to get into films and was auditioning right now and all the time, touched his cap, grinned and said, "Good afternoon, Mr. Thornton," when we passed. Thornton didn't look at him. He parked back of the place, opened his door, and stepped out.

"I can't afford this," I said.

"Wait here," Thornton said, and went away.

He came out after five minutes, carrying shallow cardboard pastry boxes. He set them on the floor back of the seat. The boxes were lined with foil, so the food was still hot when he laid plates of it on a white Bauhaus table in a bright little breakfast room next to his *Sunset* magazine kitchen. He set me in a chair that was a red leather ladle, and dropped into a duplicate across from me. On my plate were wild rice, mushroom caps and chicken in a sauce of thick cream and wine—Marsala.

"That kind of place doesn't fix food to go," I said. I know restaurants. Babe played at some good ones. For that reason I also know food. "This isn't like food to go. Also, the service was too fast. You have to cook this one order at a time. You can't keep it warm on a steam table."

The smile Thornton gave me was the kind you know is worn out but you figure you'll use it one more time before you throw it away. "I own the place," he said. "It was someone else's lunch. I preempted it. They'll have to sit through another martini. There are worse fates."

"It's good food," I said. "Thank you."

"My pleasure."

Back of Thornton were windows with red cottage curtains on brass rings. The curtains were open. There was a view of big white stucco houses with red tile roofs, on steep, well-kept, green hillsides. Just outside the window in a live-oak hung a clear plastic cylinder with a green tin lid. Hummingbirds poked their bills into holes at its base. Red syrup was inside. The birds' wings buzzed like an eight dollar radio. When there were too many birds for the number of drinking places, they charged each other and squeaked. They were pretty, but they acted mean. I was hungry as they seemed to be, and I put away the beautiful food fast.

When I looked at Thornton, he wasn't eating at all. He was hurrying to save two young ice cubes from drowning in a glass of bourbon. I had stood in the kitchen and seen him fix the drink. It hadn't involved much water. I once read a study that said bald men were seldom alcoholics—alcoholics were prone to childlike hair growth and long eyelashes. So maybe Thornton was only sorrowing, but I happen to know one habit of alcoholics, because Babe has had a few among her close admirers over the years—it was natural, wasn't it, since she worked in bars? And alcoholics tend to leave bottles standing around uncapped. Thornton's Jack Daniel's was standing out there now, losing proof. He went on with what he'd started saying in the car:

"Eric didn't like to drink. He never knew when it would make him upchuck. Also it interfered with his sexual performance. He didn't like anything to interfere with that."

"Would someone push him out a window?" I said.

"Why?" Thornton said.

"You tell me," I said. "You've known him a long time. I never knew him at all."

Thornton shook his head and finished his drink. "Too melodramatic." He stood up. "People don't push other people out of windows."

"How long did you know him?" I wondered.

"I've been trying to count." Thornton went to the kitchen. I heard the flower-paneled refrigerator door. Ice rattled into a glass. "You must have been about six months old."

I suddenly didn't want to eat any more. I folded my napkin that matched the red curtains, laid it by my plate, and stood up. Thornton came back with his glass refilled and blinked at me.

"What's wrong?"

"When I was six months old," I said, "was when Eric left Babe. And me."

Thornton nodded. "For me," he said flatly.

"Shit," I said.

"See?" Thin smile. "You didn't want to know."

He was right. I got out of there fast, through the diningroom, into the front hall with its white carpet, white door, white curve of stairs. My suitcase wasn't in sight. I panicked. "Faggot!" I yelled. "What did you do with my suitcase?"

"Keep calm." Thornton came and took the suitcase out of a white, empty little closet like a child's tomb, and handed it to me. "And don't call people names before you know what you are yourself. At your age, you can't be sure."

"I'm sure," I said. "What's the matter with this door?" I was tugging at it, but it wasn't coming open. I was so upset I didn't even see the lock. Thornton reached across me to turn it. I pushed him off. "Don't touch me." I fumbled with the lock myself. "You're not going to do to me what you did to him."

"You've got it wrong." Thornton sighed, worked the lock, opened the door. "But go on—run." His smile was wry, one-cornered. "Just do me this favor—remember that I tried to refuse."

I picked up the suitcase and walked out. A mockingbird spilled song over me from a tall eucalyptus in a yard that was a shiny slope of dark ground-ivy. I went down shallow flag steps that curved toward a street where nobody drove, where big hybiscus bushes flared red and pink at curbsides. Thornton's voice came after me:

"I asked you to find someone else."

By which he meant that I was too young and tender to face the truth. And I was just about proving him right. Because even though I believed Thornton, I was running away from him. And that was stupid, because it was too late. I knew too much now, and not enough. I stopped and turned around. Thornton was closing the door, but he saw me, and held it still.

"I want to come back," I said. "I apologize."

Thornton shrugged and looked up into the tree, narrowing his eyes against the smudged sunlight, trying to see the bird. "As you please," he said.

I went back. It was warm by now, but I didn't let Thornton take my jacket. I folded it beside me and kept the suitcase between my feet when I sat on one of the long, deep couches in a big, sunken livingroom, where everything looked as if a furniture company truck had just driven off with the wrappers. Thornton sat in an easy chair with good plain lines, beside a lamp turned on a baroque lathe, set on forged iron filigree, and gilded and crimsoned by a first-week dropout from the Tijuana School of Fine Arts.

27

He said, "I didn't know him much longer than you, really. We only lasted eight months. Then—"

"Would you go back to the start?" I said.

Thornton rubbed a hand down over his face. "Yes, all right. Babe came to work in a place I was managing—bar and restaurant. In Santa Barbara." He started to get up. "Can I get you anything? Coke? Seven-up?"

I shook my head.

He sat back and lit a cigarette. "Eric was rehearsing a play at the local little theatre. He never came into the restaurant. Until the play had finished its run. Then he came in." Thornton poked moodily at the ice cubes in his drink with a bony finger. When he looked up, his smile was wan. "I'd been reasonably happy, till that night."

"Sorry," I said. "I broke my violin."

Thornton's smile went. His voice hardened. "All right. You want the facts. The facts are as follows: he was beautiful and I wanted him, but I didn't make a pass. He was married, and I liked Babe, and they seemed happy. Of course, she ran him, but she also adored him. She was sure he had great talent, great potential. He'd be discovered, he'd have a sensational career. Meantime, he must keep acting. It didn't matter that he didn't get paid. She'd earn the living." Thornton stopped and frowned at me, blinking through his cigarette smoke. "I heard that often—all about Eric. You I didn't hear about much. Who was looking after you?"

"I don't know." I felt sorry for my baby self. "I remember a lot of women with big asses in bluejeans, with scarfs tied over their curlers, beer cans in their hands. I remember a lot of nighttime trailers, a lot of smoke from burned TV dinners. But not from that far back, I don't think. I don't know who looked after me then."

Thornton's eyes showed pity. He twisted out his cigarette, knocked back the rest of his drink, and left the room quickly. I remembered something Babe said when I annoyed her—that only people who never had kids could be soft about them. Thornton didn't look at me when he came back, just handed me a cold Coke can with the top already popped, and sat down again with another highball. This one was as dark as varnish.

"When I finally saw you," he said, "it was as a small foot sticking out of a blanket in a wicker basket. My bookkeeper was sick. I remember it was a miserable winter, lots of flu. I had to get the payroll checks out by myself. I wasn't able to do that— not on time. It was raining the morning I drove out to find that trailer camp and hand Babe her week's wages. I thought I saw her pass me, heading the other direction, maybe to the restaurant to find me—but she was traveling fast, and visibility was bad, and I couldn't be sure it was her. I didn't turn around and try to follow.

"Eric was alone in the trailer. He didn't want company, but it was raining, so he felt he had to ask me inside. He mumbled apologies for how the place looked. Nothing was wrong with the basic housekeeping, but there was broken crockery on the floor. And sections of the coffee maker, one of the metal kind. Coffee and grounds all over.

Eric was shaking. He was white around mouth too. I've never known anyone else that happens to when they get upset."

"Me," I said, "if it's bad enough."

"It was bad this time." Thornton laughed without sound, grimly. "He offered me a cup of coffee—just to be saying words, you know? Reflex manners. I stared at the dented parts on the floor. He turned red and picked them up, muttering something about an accident. He didn't fit them together. He dropped them into the sink. 'Ah, hell,' he said. 'Let's go out and get a cup someplace.' But you were there, sound asleep, with that miniature foot sticking out of the blanket. There'd obviously been one hell of a row, but it hadn't bothered you."

"So what happened?" I said.

"We didn't go out," Thornton said.

"You got it on—right?" I tried to sound detached.

"Do you want the details?" Thornton looked skeptical.

I did and I didn't. I didn't say yes. But I didn't say no. Maybe I nodded. Thornton took a breath and went on:

"He started to cry, sat down on the bed, bunk, whatever you call it, and held his head in his hands, and sobbed as if—"

"—his heart would break," I said. "Why?"

Thornton had loosened his tie. Now he jerked it off and dropped it on the floor beside his chair. He unfastened another button on his shirt. Two. His chest was hairless, smooth, flat as a little kid's.

"Post-coital depression, I believe it's called. Only it had reached a chronic stage with Eric. It had gotten so he turned on Babe every time afterward. He didn't have, didn't need, anything to fight about. He fought. Savagely. He couldn't figure it out, but he couldn't stop himself. Babe didn't know what it meant, either, but she was tired of it. And he didn't blame her."

"But you knew," I said.

"You might stop sneering," Thornton said.

"I'm young and easily embarrassed," I said.

Thornton gave his bleak little smile. "That's Babe's sense of humor. Eric didn't have one." He looked into his whiskey and nodded. "But yes, I did know." He swallowed from the glass. "But you're careful, if you're wise. You don't assume anything. It's an old homosexual failing—to think someone's available because you want them."

"How old were you?" I said.

"Twenty-five, but I'm a fast learner." Thornton studied me thoughtfully. "I had better sense then than now."

I wasn't sure what that meant but I didn't like it. "Go on," I said, and swallowed some of the Coke.

"He was miserable. I felt sorry for him. I touched him—his hair, I guess. It was beautiful hair. Snow white." He looked away. "Like yours."

"Oh, boy," I said.

"Sorry." Thornton shook his head quickly and drank. "He took hold of my hand and held onto it. I sat down next to him and put my arm over his shoulders. It—happened very quickly, after that." Thornton's smile belonged to a long time ago. "Afterward, we lay there warm together, holding each other, with only the sound of the rain on the metal roof of that trailer. "And"—his chuckle was smug—"there was no post-coital depression. He said he'd never been so happy. I knew I hadn't."

"Was it his first time doing it with another dude?"

"If I give you the answer, you'll hit me with it," Thornton said. "Next question."

He was juiced. It sounded like *nesskweshn*.

"I can't picture it," I said, "I really can't."

Thornton set his drink down and stood up. His hand went to the fourth button on the shirt. I stared at it coldly and it stopped. "No," Thornton said, and dropped into the chair again. "We were not as young as you." He articulated carefully now. "But we were young. We are no longer—" He failed to make the G hard and went back and tried the word over. "Longer. We are no longer young. I couldn't make you see it."

"Did I wake up?" I asked. The human mind interests me. I have a good memory. I keep wondering how far back it goes, why a person wouldn't remember right back to the start, being born, or even before, when they're still inside their mother. Thornton didn't help.

"Eric had you on his knee, spooning something yellow and mushy out of a little jar into your little pink mouth, when Babe came back."

"Did you tell her?"

Thornton winced. "Next question."

"You were together eight months. Where?"

"Here. Los Angeles. I'd had an offer to take over

a restaurant down here. Eric wanted to try for pictures. We came down together, took an apartment together. There'd been small blond actors who'd made it before. Alan Ladd. John Lund. He didn't see why his size should hurt him. It did. It was the era of the big uglies—Mitchum, Palance. Charm, suav—" He had trouble with that word too. He tried some more Jack Daniel's. "Suavity, grace, cultivated speech were no longer at a premium. It didn't matter to me whether he got work or not. I was making good money. He felt differently." Thornton made a wry face. "His so-called break came at Christmas, Christmas eve. I lost track of him at a party, in a house about five times as pretentious as this one, and God knows, this is preten—" He couldn't manage it twice. I helped him.

"Pretentious enough," I said.

Thornton shut his eyes and nodded. "And when I located him, it was in a remote bedroom with a well-known director of, at that time, sixty years of age, at least—who had promised him the second lead in something large and glossy concerning—" He waved a hand. "Ah, who cares what it concerned?"

"Doctors," I said, "hospitals. *The Healing Blade.* Fox. Technicolor. It wasn't a very big part."

"The kind you get that way seldom are." Thornton drew a deep breath in through his nose and let it out slowly. He wasn't focusing well. He shut and opened his eyes and gave a weary smile. "I told him so. He didn't like it, but when I turned out to be right, he swore he'd never let it happen again. Understand, I didn't hold it against him. I knew he was dying to work. I knew he loved me.

33

The old man meant nothing. But—" Thornton sighed and slumped lower in the chair, long thin legs stretched straight out, crossed at the ankles. He set the drink on his gaunt belly, staring at it, turning it. "Someone came along, someone in the business, who could help him and did help him. An agent, Toddy Niles. What started as the casting-couch gambit turned into love. It was honest and real, and I was out."

"You cried at the cemetery," I said. "How come? It was seventeen years ago."

"He came back. Life is long, and not long at all. Doors close, but they don't lock. People once very big in your life are going to come back." He nodded his bald head with heavy gravity. "Remember that."

"Yes, sir," I said.

Thornton blinked. "Where was I?"

"He came back," I said. "Lately?"

"Last winter."

"And it started over?" There was something weird about it. I couldn't picture them together, naked, when they were in their twenties. In their forties? It made me a little sick. "You got it on with each other again?"

Thornton tilted the glass at his mouth but there was only ice left. He pushed up out of the chair and moved away, being careful about his balance. The Coke was too sweet, and I wanted to be rid of it, so I went after him. Also I was afraid he might fall down. He didn't fall down, and I poured the Coke quietly down the sink while his back was turned. Building another highball, he missed, and three ice cubes hit the floor and ran from each other. I picked them up, washed them off, and dropped them into Thornton's glass.

"Thank you," he said, and to himself, solemnly, "thank you." He filled the jigger from the bottle. A lot of whiskey puddled on the counter, but some got into his glass. "And thank you for coming to your father's funeral." He swung to the sink and opened the tap over the glass and shut it again right away. He turned to me. "And thank you for coming here."

"Thank you," I said. "I know more about him now."

"Ah," Thornton said dejectedly, "I haven't told you anything. How beautiful he was. How kind. How thoughtful. The soft sound of his voice. How well he chose words. How wonderful it was to look up—oh, in the restaurant, say—and see him coming toward you smiling, with his hair shining. How good it was to go places with him, and feel everyone staring. As if you'd trained an angel to walk on a leash."

"And how long," I said, "did it last this time?"

Thornton flinched. "I'm sorry for you," he said, out of a tight throat. "All of you. Your whole generation, and your awful disenchantment."

"I was never enchanted," I said.

"All right, all right." He nodded, eyes shut again. "Wrong word. How about cynicism?"

"What you're trying not to say," I told him, "is that it didn't last very long."

"We met a few times. Hotels, motels. They were good times, tender, loving. They"—Thornton lifted and dropped a hand—"just ended. He didn't call when he was supposed to call. I couldn't find him, didn't know where he lived. When he cropped up again, there was someone new—someone, I gathered, quite young."

"You mean, like, recently? Just before he died? Who? Didn't he give you a name?"

Thornton answered bitterly, "I didn't ask."

"I better go." I started out of the kitchen.

"Wait." Thornton's glass clicked on the counter. I turned in the doorway, and he gripped my shoulders. "You said you couldn't picture it." His speech was under control suddenly, and his eyes made sense. "I want you to know what it was like. It was very beautiful." His fingers started to work on the knot of my tie. I pushed him back.

"It's not my thing," I said.

Thornton opened his hands and looked down into them. "It's very lonely in the world—" he began.

"You're right." I walked out and he followed.

"—When people go out of it forever," he finished.

"Maybe it's lonelier for them," I said.

Thornton caught my arm. "I won't be taking anything from you. You'll still have it. I only want you"—there were tears in his eyes—"to be Eric for me. Just now, today. Just now, that he's gone and cold in the ground. To show me—to show me that it isn't all that lonely in the world. And to show you—"

I pried his fingers loose. "I can't." I picked up my jacket and suitcase and went around him standing there slump-shouldered, miserable. I climbed the two steps into the hall and pulled open the door. The crazy bird was still pouring music

into the killer air. I tried to shut the door, but
Thornton had hold of it. I went fast down the flag
steps.

"Are you going back to Babe?" he called.

I stopped and turned. "I won't take her your
love."

"You don't understand," he said sadly, shaking
his head. "You don't understand at all."

"Nobody understands anybody," I said.

I wanted Gus.

Venice beach. I hadn't known there were really
canals there. They looked fake, not deep enough
to float anything, the water dark and greasy.
Bridges humped over them, gray stucco, broken
in places so you could see the chickenwire and tar-
paper underneath. Ducks swam in the canals. Dogs
and little kids ran along their broken cement edges.
Now and then a fish jumped.

The afternoon was hot. Gulls fell like scraps of
china from a blue tablecloth sky. I was lost. I kept
switching the suitcase from hand to hand. Sweat
trickled into my eyes when I tried to read the little
faded streetsigns that marked alleyways too nar-
row for cars, between bat and board cottages. The
cottages were old but not shabby. They'd been
painted lately, bright pinks, greens, yellows—and
they had new, silvery roofing. The place looked
like a Disneyland discard.

A dozen thin young cats cried at a screendoor,
and a fat old woman in hip-high rubber boots and
a man's hat came out with two plates and set them
down. If that was what she was, she was the only

human I had seen so far, not counting the kids. I leaned on a lavender wooden gate, whose paint came off chalky on my suit, and asked her how to find Poppy Court. The cats squalled, fighting over the food on the plates, but I didn't have any trouble hearing her. They could probably hear her in Pasadena.

"What do you want with Poppy Court? Full of hippies. You don't look like any hippie. Nice boy like you—you don't want to get messed up with that kind. All that dope and drink and sex and all that?"

"No," I said. "I've come to save my sister."

Her smile had more creases than an origami instruction book. "Why sure you have." She hoisted a few cats out of her way with a big rubber-covered foot and came waddling at me with her arms out. "Bless your heart, of course you have, Lord love you."

I backed off.

But she didn't hug me. She dug into her bulging hip pocket and tugged out a wad of printed paper. Bible tracts. She pushed them into my hands. "You give her these to read. Poor things. They don't know Jesus died for them. Listen"— she shoved her pink walrus face at me, wobbling her chins, very earnest—"I don't hate them. Pshaw, no. I feel sorry for them. They're looking, seeking. They're lost. Nothing to believe in. All those crazy foreign religions. It's sad, when Jesus is just waiting to love them."

"Very sad," I said. "Where's Poppy Court?"

"You give those to your poor, lost sister," she said.

"If you tell me how to find her," I said.

It involved two bridges I'd already crossed. Off the first one I dropped the tracts into the canal. Ducks swam over, but they didn't want them either. Before I saw the Poppy Court sign, I saw the second van parked next to a bright blue cottage beside the canal. Then I saw the fat man's derby with the flower decal on top. He was siting in his mangy body hair and a pair of ragged shorts, with his legs pretzeled, on the blue stoop. He held his hands flattened together in front of his whiskery lips, and his eyes, behind the steelrim glasses, looked far away.

"Om," I said. "Incháláh."

But he didn't pay any attention.

"I'm looking for Gus," I said.

No answer. I shrugged. The door was open. I edged past the fat man and went inside. The room was long and lowceilinged, with a big round table at its center—a table top, actually, set on bricks or something, that held it only about a foot off the floor. There was a runny Madras cloth on it, a thick, rainbow-colored candle, a harmonica, a paperback book on how to survive in the woods, and a shellacked half-gallon tincan with the label removed that held cattails, pussywillows, and glass flowers on long wire stems.

There were no chairs. On the floor lay rolled-up mattresses wrapped in gaudy cotton cloth, Indian, Japanese. Posters of rock album covers were Scotch taped to the walls, along with some children's wax crayon drawings, and a blownup photo of a marijuana plant printed in green. A sitar, missing its strings, and with a hole poked in its gourd end, leaned above a fireplace where an old gas heater squatted. A guitar case gaped empty in a corner. Someplace I could barely hear, someone was playing the guitar.

A curtain of bright wooden beads hung in a square archway at the room's end. I rattled through it into a smaller room where the daylight came in only dimly, dyed dark oranges and reds by more of the bleeding Madras cloth hung across the windows. There were microphones on shiny stands, amplifiers, big black loudspeakers, more guitar cases, and what seemed to be an electronic organ. Someone was breathing snuffily. I smelled menthol.

"Gus?" I said softly.

But it wasn't Gus. On the floor in a corner on a mattress covered with a blanket lay a little kid about seven with curly yellow hair. He was asleep on his back in a twisted T-shirt and Levi's, breathing cold germs noisily in and out through his open mouth. Beyond him was a swing door to which was taped a blownup photo of a dead, oil-slick-smothered sea bird. I pushed the door and stepped into greasy heat.

Hughie was in the kitchen, stirring what looked like spaghetti sauce in a frying pan big enough to play football in. He wore a leather hat and fat blue beads and old denims patched at the knees. He looked at me with shiny, bloodshot eyes, and lifted a dripping wooden spoon out of the sauce and saluted me with it. "Alan," he said. The guitar was easier to hear now, someplace outside, thoughtful, maybe sad.

"Hi," I said.

Hughie laughed low in his throat. "Oh, man, high is where it's at. High, high, high." He spun slowly around. "Wow! Everybody else is on downers. But not responsible Hughie. We got to eat. Solemn occasions await us." He nodded, looking very grave. "Tonight we got a gig. Like, for bread, baby. For bread. Anyway, when we got back, this place looked terrible." He made a sour face, and gestured at the old but very shiny white sink. "Like, dirty dishes up to here. Ants. Roaches. Garbage. Like, Piper is a genius, writes great songs, man. But dust, and all that shit? He never even sees it. Jesus, the kids were so raunchy you couldn't tell them apart. So"—he sighed good-naturedly—"somebody had to clean up, man. Yeah." He frowned and bent over the sauce, sniffing. "Does it smell like it's burning to you?"

"A little," I said.

"A little is too many." Hughie shifted the big skillet, and picked up an unused grill off the back burner, and set it on top of the front grill, where the fire was a thin, blue circle. He balanced the pan on the stacked grills. "There. That'll keep her sweet."

"Where's Gus," I asked.

"Asleep, sacked out. Everybody's sacked out except the kids." He cranked open a can of black olives and drained it into the sink. "Gus is in the back bedroom. That's hers and—"

"And what?"

Hughie chuckled and emptied the olives into the spaghetti sauce. "And that's where she is." He jerked his head. "You got into the hall through the diningroom. I think you can squeeze past the equipment. Then just follow the hall."

I followed the hall. The door of the back room wasn't quite shut. I pushed it and put my head inside. A mattress lay on the floor with sheets on it. The windows here were curtained in yellow cotton, moving a little in air that smelled of warm ocean, but I could see a figure under the top sheet. And the hair, the long brown hair spread out as if in water—that was Gus's hair. I dropped my jacket and tie, crouched to pry off my shoes, peel off my socks, and crossed the cool bare floor to her, unbuttoning my shirt. The guitar sounded close here, musing, mournful. I sat down on the matresss.

"Mmm?" Gus stirred.

"It's me," I said, and tossed the shirt away, and turned and kissed her mouth.

"Hi." She said it sleepily and smiled without opening her eyes. Her arms came around me.

"Just a second." I finished getting naked and then I was under the sheet with her, and she was naked too, so that was fine, and I hugged her hard, and fought to keep from crying, I was so relieved to be here, to find her here. She hadn't given me the address. I'd talked it out of the dude who had driven the rescue van. Inside Gus's thin chest, her heart moved like someone in a dark house not wanting to waken people. There was a film of salty summer afternoon sweat on her little breasts when I tasted them. She laughed, softly, from far off. Her eyelids fluttered, then opened. And she didn't laugh anymore. She lay stiff, frowning. Then she sat up. Suddenly. Back against the wall. Eyes wide. "Oh, no!"

I knelt up. "What do you mean—'oh, no'?"

"You're not Piper," she said.

"I'm Alan," I said. "We did it on the beach this morning. Remember?"

"Oh, listen—" She gulped and scrambled to her feet, scared, shaking her head. "You—you better go."

"Why?" I stood up too. "I told you I love you."

"No, you shouldn't have come here." She grabbed up my shirt and tried to put it on me, fumbling, frantic. "You have to go—right away!"

"Why?" I caught her hands. "I meant what I said."

"Oh, God," she moaned. "Look, will you please get dressed." She snatched up my pants and shorts. "Come *on*, come *on!*"

But it was too late. A voice spoke. From the window. We both looked. A young man had pushed his head through the curtains. Yellow hair. Frontier mustache.

"What the hell's going on?" he said.

He said it mildly, in a country-western accent, and with a slow, country-western smile. He pushed a guitar carefully through the curtains, leaned it against the wall inside, and then began to climb over the windowsill. His shoulders were wide and bony. He wore a green leather vest with fringes.

I stared. "Who are you?"

"It goes the other way around, friend." The heel of his cowboy boot snagged on the curtain and he sprawled at our feet—our naked, childlike, guilty-looking little feet. "Excuse me." He got up, brushed off his knees, stood straight, and looked down at me from six feet up. His expression was amiable, but his eyes were empty. "Who are you?" He shed the leather vest.

"Alan," Gus said. "He hitched a ride with us this morning—from Goleta or someplace." She pulled the long dress on over her head. It muffled her lies. "I thought he might need a place to crash." Her head appeared, she shook out her hair. "So I told him we had room. He came. He got in bed with me. I was asleep. I thought it was you."

"Aw, now, Gus, that just can't be true." His laugh was a gentle reproach. It scared me. "Look at him. How tall are you, little buddy?"

"Seven feet two," I said. "I'm Kareem Abdul Jabbar, only somebody put bleach in my bubble bath."

"Excuse me if I don't laugh," he said. "Finding your old lady naked with some dude also naked in his conjugal bed don't make a man feel too humorous."

"Piper," Gus wailed, "I told you. I was asleep. It was a mistake."

"Not mine," I said, and poked an arm into my shirt.

Piper yanked the shirt off me and tossed it into a corner. He sat on the floor and pushed his boots off and unbuckled his belt. I started after my shirt. Piper caught my ankle. I looked down at him. His

44

eyes still didn't smile. "You come to get it on with her, didn't you?"

I glanced at Gus. She shook her head desperately. Piper was busy pushing off his pants and didn't see her, but evidently he didn't need to. "Don't pay her no mind," he told me. "I know how it went. In Hughie's van, you can't breathe without you get stoned. And when Gus gets stoned, she reaches for just one thing. It don't matter what size it is." His looked about a foot long.

Gus said, "You could have been there."

"Could have and should have." Piper nodded, sighed, and got to his feet. "But I wasn't." He slung a long, hard arm over my shoulders, another over Gus's shoulders, and laughed softly down at her. "And two of them is bound to be better than one." He turned me a grin. "Even if it don't amount to much." He squeezed my shoulder, trying to get me to laugh with him, but it was my turn now not to feel humorous.

"I'm going," I said, and bent for my shorts. I didn't get them. Piper put a long foot on my ass and shoved, and I somersaulted onto the mattress. Before I could get up, Gus fell on top of me, and Piper threw himself on top of both of us, holding us down. His forearm came across my windpipe. "Hey," I coughed. "No. Get off. Look, I didn't know—"

Piper was ripping Gus's dress off over her head, while inside the dress she pounded at him with little girl fists and gave small, soft screams. The dress went flying, like a kite without sticks. Piper shoved her back into the corner and held her there with a big hand while he straddled my chest, kneeling on my arms. All I could do was use my knees to play bongos on his back. It didn't faze him.

"Don't tucker yourself like that," he said gently, concerned. "You come here for something better. All in the world I want is for you to have it." He got off me slowly, watching me as if I were a live grenade. "Gus?" he said in that sweet, cajoling, down-homey voice. "You do what you was about to do before I popped in the window."

She shook her head. He reached for her. She bit her lip and kicked him in the stomach. It looked like a hard kick, but he had a belly like a washboard, and he didn't even wince. He gave that soft, dangerous little Nashville laugh of his, and reached for her. I rolled away, crawled half a length toward the window. I didn't care about clothes now. All I wanted was to get out. I didn't. But while Piper was tackling me and dragging me back, Gus did. Out the room door. I heard it slam, heard her little heels pounding off down the hallway.

"Gus!" I howled. Actually, I only began to howl it. Because Piper flipped me on my face on the mattress. No, he didn't stomp me. He did something else that hurt, holding my face in the pillows while he did it, so the only yell anyone could have heard was when it ended and he yelled, "Wahoo!" like I was a rodeo calf he'd bulldogged. Or his first gold record.

A minute later, I was standing up to my ass in the canal with weeds and mud slippery under my feet, and Piper was throwing my clothes at me, and I was trying to catch them, and missing, and falling down in the sunset-bloody water, and wanting to cry because my suit that cost Babe like a hundred dollars was someplace in the muck now, with my good shoes, and I was splashing around, grabbing my shorts and T-shirt that were worth, like, fifty-nine cents each, and trying to get to my feet again, and slipping again, and getting my sinuses full of greasy water, and gagging and choking, and getting up just in time to save the suitcase before it could sink.

Piper wouldn't let me come back on shore, so I began slogging along in the water, holding the suitcase to my chest, while Piper followed on the bank, jeering. I figured everybody in town would be down to look at the two of us, stark naked, but they must have been eating, or watching television, or maybe deaf or stoned, or had a lot more experience minding their own business than most people. No one came. Even the dogs had gone someplace else. Even the ducks. I didn't look at Piper. I waded on. Piper ran out of things to call me. And when I reached the bridge and looked back, Piper was nowhere to be seen.

Slipping and sliding in duck shit, I climbed out of the canal. On dry weeds I laid the suitcase and squatted to open it, when I heard the sound of a car coming. I was in a vacant lot. About twenty feet away, an old car sat rotting on flat tires. I threw myself at it, yanked open a rusty back door, fell onto ripped and gritty upholstery. Cars came over the bridge like ducks in a shooting gallery. I snapped open the suitcase, kicked into my white

Levi's, got a T-shirt on backward, pulled on tube socks and Adidas, flapped into my red jacket, shut the suitcase and got out of there.

Not at a run. The way Piper had used me, I felt lucky to be able to hobble. Three sick blocks later, ready to pass out from the pain, I pushed a tin door marked MEN. But mirrors in service station restrooms are too high. I couldn't figure a way to look at the damage. All my hand told me was there was blood. My folding money, the few dollars left after the taxi trip to the cemetery, was in my suit at the bottom of the canal. I couldn't pay a doctor to look at me. There was change in my jacket pocket. I limped to a bus-stop. Hitching rides had lost its appeal for me.

Luckily, the bus that came wasn't crowded, because I didn't feel like standing up. Or sitting, either. I lay on my side along the wide rear seat in the vibrations and fumes of the engine. It took two long-haul buses to get me to the street I wanted. When I got off the second bus, it was night. I stood in the red and yellow blink of a neon sign on the front of a corner tavern, and squinted up the steep twist of Westerly Terrace into the dark. And knew I couldn't climb it.

I found a phone booth. My luck, if you want to call it that, held. Thorton was at home. He even sounded sober. I limped back to the corner and propped myself with both hands on the back of the bus bench, with my head bowed and my eyes shut. I didn't like Thornton, but I had nobody else in L.A. to turn to. I just hoped to God he'd keep his hands off. I kept making up smart remarks to slap him with.

But when the Bentley slid to the curb in front of the waiting bench five minutes later, and the door swung open, and I gritted my teeth and eased myself down on the seat, did I use any of those smart remarks? Did I even say anything? Hell, no. I cried. I knew what was wrong with me. I was in pain and I was tired. Trying to catch rides and missing them all night, I hadn't slept, or on the beach after the wreck, either, or even in the van getting to L.A. Also my stomach was empty. So I had excuses for bawling—honest ones.

They didn't help. I was disgusted with myself, spilling my ravished innocence story between wet kindergarten sobs, to a man I hated, the man who'd taken my father away from me. A fag, at that. But what really disturbed me was wanting what I wanted. I wanted Thornton, for Christ sake, to put his arms around me. If he had done it, I would have gone crazy, but it was what I wanted. If I hadn't been so busy with grief and rage, I'd have thrown up. I really despised myself.

Thornton didn't put his arms around me. He turned off the symphony broadcast he'd had going on the radio, in order to hear me talk, but he didn't say a word. He drove up the crooked hill with both hands on the wheel and eyes front. The Bentley dipped into a cement ramp on the downhill side of his house, and the garage door lifted by itself on a clean, well-lighted place, like an empty theatre stage. When the Bentley was inside, the door shut itself with hardly a sound. It made me nervous.

Thornton got from behind the wheel and came around to help me out, but I didn't want the man

49

touching me, and I was already on my feet. Getting there made me feel like Piper was doing it to me all over again. I grabbed the door to steady myself. I must have looked pale.⁴ I felt pale. Thornton took the suitcase out of my hand and carried it to a side door. He opened the door and set the suitcase inside, and I took a couple of shaky steps, trying to follow him.

He came back, said, "Don't panic," bent at the knees and picked me up. I didn't panic. I didn't exactly relax, but I didn't panic. Thornton carried me inside, up some patterned tile stairs, through the house where music whispered from a stereo, and into a small, neat room—a maid's room, I guessed, past the kitchen, past the laundry. He laid me down on a bed and helped me out of the jacket and hung it on a chair. He had switched on a ceiling light with his elbow as we'd come through the door. The light gleamed on his bald head.

"I'll call a doctor," he said.

"I can't afford a doctor," I said.

Thornton went away. He brought back whiskey in a squat glass, and three aspirins to kill the pain. Liquor was never on my fun list. I'd been raised wrong. Other children got cute little party tastes of daddy's martini or mama's margarita, but not Babe Tarr's kid. A customer in a bar where she worked could get slapped silly, offering me booze. But I choked down what Thornton brought me, and the aspirins too. I handed back the glass.

"Anyway," I said, "doctors don't make house calls anymore. It's a well-worn subject of television wit."

"This one will," he said. "He's a friend."

"Another queer?" I asked.

"See?" He twitched a smile. "You're feeling better already."

The doctor wore brown tweed with a jacket that tightened at the waist and flared in the skirts. He was short and tubby and about fifty. White bushy sideburns, rosy cheeks, twinkling Santa Claus eyes. The suit belonged on somebody twenty years old in the wonderful world of show business, but he acted like a doctor. He pried off my shoes, dragged my pants down, rolled me over like a carcass in a butcher-shop, and punctured my butt with a needle.

"Get under the covers," he said. "Relax."

He went out then, and talked with Thornton for a while in the kitchen. I couldn't make out the words, but once I heard the doctor laugh. It made me want to leave. But when the doctor came back, all he did was fold the covers down and gently probe the damage. It hurt, I thought, but the bourbon and aspirin and whatever had been in that hypodermic made it seem like yesterday's pain or a dead actor's scream from a movie on the late show. The doctor took a thing in crackly plastic from his kit and unwrapped it and slipped it inside me like microfilm in a spy novel. He patted my ass, stood up, pulled the covers back over me, went into a little bathroom, and splashed water. In the doorway, drying his hands, he grinned.

"You'll be all right," he said. "You're more—"

"Don't tell me," I said, "let me guess. 'More scared than hurt'?"

"Or words to that effect." The doctor hung the towel back and clicked off the bathroom light.

"I have an explanation," I said. "It's not exactly something that happens to me every day—okay?"

His kit was on a rattan basket chair. He shut it, picked it up. "It happens to somebody."

"You talk like a doctor," I said.

"Some people," he said, "even get to like it."

"Oh, wow!" I put my face in the pillow.

"Sleep it off," the doctor said, and switched out the light and shut the door.

It should have been easy. I was drugged out of my bright little mind. I shut my eyes. Piper was with me, bony, naked, grinning that grin of his. His cock was like a two-by-four. I opened my eyes and rolled onto my back. A window showed me stars, the black ragged curve of a hill, the lonesome lights of a car climbing, till it got lost. My eyes fell shut again. My father stood at the end of a hospital corridor in a surgeon's gown and cap. The camera closed in on him. He pulled the mask down so it hung around his neck. He gave a weary smile. *Congratulations,* he said, *it's a faggot.*

"You're the faggot," I said, and turned on my side.

"That's very much on your mind, isn't it?"

I fluttered my eyes. Thornton stood thin in the doorway, with far light behind him, and a glass in his hand.

"Considering what's happened to me," I said, "I don't think that's too surprising."

"What happened to you was rape." Thornton

came and stood by the bed. "Don't confuse that with what goes on between—men who love each other. Piper was punishing you. He was angry and he wanted to give you pain. It was just an act of aggression. He wasn't gay."

"Look," I said, "I really appreciate all you've done for me. I'll pay you back. But not the way you want. I'm sorry."

Thornton gave a sad, quiet laugh. "You're so like Eric." The ice cubes tinkled in his glass and he sat on the bed. The bed wasn't that wide. It would have taken an accident for us not to touch. I moved my legs. "So like Eric. He was as frightened as you. That was the reason he'd married Babe. He couldn't face being—different."

"I better sleep," I said, and turned my back.

He put a hand on my thigh. There were blankets and a sheet between the hand and me but it made me feel naked and scared. It also made me feel sexy, and that made me angry. "I'd like you to know," Thornton said, "how it really is—gentle and tender and good."

"I'm not Eric," I said. "He's dead—remember?"

Thornton let the hand move lightly down my thigh to the knee and back up while he said, "Lying out there in the cold and dark with no one to hold him, and no one for him to hold. Alone. Forever."

"Department of original thoughts," I said.

His hand stopped moving.

" 'It's an old homosexual failing,' " I quoted him, " 'to think somebody's available because you want them'."

"You're just afraid." The hand moved again,

down slowly to my foot. It held my foot. I liked the feeling and hated myself for liking it. "Young and afraid. And love is nothing to be afraid of."

I got my own hand from under the covers, took his hand and gave it back to him. "It wouldn't work," I said. "I'm not like him. Babe is fine with me." Then I remembered something and I squinted at Thornton, sitting shadowy in his white shirt, shoulders slumped. "Hotels," I said. "Motels. Why? Why not here?"

He sighed. "I don't live alone." He stood up. "Did you think I'd been celibate all those years?"

"Then what did you need with Eric?" I asked. "What do you need with me?"

"When you've lived with someone that long, you'll understand." Thornton moved to the door. "There's a lot of irony in this, isn't there? Imagine how Babe will feel, knowing you came to me, of all people, for help."

"I'll be sure to tell her," I said.

His laugh was bleak. "Good night," he said, and went out and shut the door.

Canal water must have got into my Timex, because it wouldn't tell me how early or late it was when I woke up. It was daylight. I eased out of bed, ready for pain, but there wasn't too much left. Just a reminder. I used the toilet with considerable worry, but everything worked. I wasn't damaged for life. When I was in the shower, someone began beating on the door and shouting. The noise of the water was so loud, I couldn't understand the words, but the tone was angry. I splashed the soap off, cranked the shower handles, and listened.

"Come out of there," the voice said, "right now."

It wasn't Thornton. Then I heard Thornton.

"You're behaving like an idiot."

"Good." The pounding stopped. "Then you won't feel quite so lonely."

"He's just a child. He didn't have anywhere else to go. He doesn't know anyone in L.A. He hasn't any money—"

"Like father, like son," the voice said, and the knuckles worked on the wood again. "Come on. Open up. That bathroom is half mine, and I want you out of it."

There was an opaque window. I slid the panel back and looked out. No luck. I was on the steep side of the house. A treetop was below, a jacaranda, feathery leaves, purple flowers. It cast moving shadows on the hard, clean, white cement garage ramp twenty feet farther down. But even if the window were next to the ground, all I had to wear was my T-shirt. I gave up, pulled the T-shirt on, and said through the door:

"May I please have my pants?"

The voice made a remark that reflected adversely on my chastity and Thornton's presumed detailed knowledge of my anatomy and of his, the voice's, total disinterest, so I unlocked the door and stepped out.

The voice belonged to a man younger than Thornton. He was short and blond. His white shirt had short sleeves, and his arms looked thick and hard. Thornton stood beside him, wearing a pained expression. He held out my Levi's to me.

"Jack de Hooch," he said. "Alan Tarr."

De Hooch stared me up and down with cold, pale blue eyes. "Good God," he said.

"I know." The Levi's had lain on the floor all

night. I shook out the wrinkles. "I look like my father."

"Dangerously," de Hooch said. "You'd better go carefully if you plan to stay in Los Angeles."

I paused with one leg in the Levi's. I hadn't dried off from the shower, but I didn't think that was why I felt cold. "What's that supposed to mean?"

"That you could be killed before someone realised you weren't him. He."

"Will you please," Thornton said, "shut up?"

"I was only telling him for his own protection," de Hooch said. He had a nasty smile.

"Wait a second." I tottered a little, getting into the other pantleg. "What do you mean—someone?"

De Hooch shrugged. "Almost anyone who knew him. To know him was to want to kill him."

I buttoned my fly and looked at Thornton. "And you told me people don't push people out of windows."

"It would have been my pleasure," de Hooch said.

"You're talking too much," Thornton said.

"Possibly." De Hooch went out of the room. "I want my coffee."

"You were under sedation." Thornton picked up my jacket from the back of the rattan chair. "I thought you'd sleep till he was out of the house."

"You should have told me." I sat on the bed to put on my shoes. The motion reminded me of where I was wounded. "He heard the toilet flush, right? He heard the shower?"

"He'd never have come in here otherwise."

Thornton did something to the jacket, maybe tried to brush the stain off the sleeve. "You were safe in here."

"I don't feel safe." I stood in my shoes and Thornton held the jacket for me and I backed into it.

"Pretend to leave," he said under his breath. "You can come back in, say, an hour."

"Forget it," I said, and de Hooch was in the room again with a mug in his hand. I told him, "I'm going home."

"You couldn't have thought of that last night?"

"I didn't do anything wrong," I said.

His smile didn't believe me. "You're very young."

"But not very queer," I said.

"You're identical with Eric in every other way, including coming begging to Glen Thornton when you're on your ass. You're queer, all right."

"Begging?" I looked at Thornton. "Did he get money from you?"

"Actors don't have steady incomes," he said.

"All those hotels and motels," I said. "I thought it was a secret."

De Hooch laughed like a trap closing. "It's not easy to keep secrets with a joint back account."

"A lot of money?" I asked.

De Hooch cocked his head and blinked. "Four five hundred dollar checks. Why do you ask?"

I said to Thornton, "Did he pay you back?"

Thornton tried to smile. "Don't worry about it."

"My God," de Hooch marveled. "How very like he is! Look at the pain in the child's eyes, the sincerity. You just *know* he's going to earn that money selling newspapers in the snow, and pay you back every cent." The steel trap laugh snapped again. "Until he walks out that door."

"Hold it." Thornton eyed de Hooch suspiciously. "When did you meet Eric? You claimed you'd never seen him."

De Hooch drank coffee.

"Where did you see him?" Thornton shouted. "When?"

De Hooch talked to me. "Understand something. I have lived with Glen Thornton for thirteen years. Everything we own, we own together, house, business, automobiles, insurance, future, everything. I also happen to love him. The only one who could threaten any of it was your father. Yesterday he was buried. I could breathe. Then you turn up. Do I make myself clear?"

"I'm walking out that door," I said. And I did.

The building was tall and white and glossy in the morning sun. It stood at the top of a long slide of white cement boulevard that looked like the one Thornton had driven me down yesterday to his restaurant—his and de Hooch's. I pushed through heavy glass doors into a lobby forty feet high where a bronze starburst sculpture hung with tiny colored lights flickering in it like symptoms of eternal decay.

I studied the building directory, plastic letters behind polished plate glass. The name wasn't there under N, and I wondered if for once I had forgotten something. I didn't think so, not numbers, anyway, read from a telephone directory. I read the list slowly from the top. The name was there, finally, with ten others, a subhead under World-wide Foremost Agency. I let an elevator suck me up to the eighth floor and stepped out into a Tar-zan jungle of philodendrons. But civilization wasn't far off—deep-grained wood paneling, couches and chairs in rubbed gold brown velveteen, a carpet you waded in.

In a corner was a counter not quite as tall as I am. I went and stood on tiptoe and looked over it. A young woman was there in a Roaring Twenties dress and a little cap of smooth black hair like a boy's. She was too pretty to be real. I didn't want to say anything. I wanted to climb over the barrier and hug her. There was a big, white, pillowy ear-phone attached to one side of her head. She was a Planet Stories girl, that was the control-panel of this fourteen-story-tall space ship, and she was lis-tening to countdown. In a minute, she and I would cancel gravity, lift off faster than the speed of light, to hurtle forever through the cold, black endless-ness of space—alone, locked together naked on one of those couches over there. The New Adam. The New Eve. Her star-map eyes smiled.

"Good morning. May I help you?"

"Toddy Niles," I said.

"Theodore." She plugged in. We didn't lift off.

"It used to be Toddy," I said.

She smiled again. "You don't look that old." Her smile turned regretful. "I should warn you, he doesn't see new talent without an appointment."

"I don't have any talent," I said. "Tell him it's Alan Tarr—Eric Tarr's son."

She told someone, unplugged the thing and said, "Will you be seated, please? He'll see you in a moment."

I walked off to do what she asked. I would always, all my life long, do anything she told me. I started to sit down, being careful of my ass. But there wasn't time. A woman like a find from the Valley of the Kings came through a combed cedar door, switched on a smile, and said, "Mr. Tarr? This way, please." She had a very nice baritone, and red claws.

I thought the doctor's clothes last night were high style. When I saw Niles I knew I'd been wrong. His shirt collar was so high that when he talked, you expected a ten second delay for the sound to reach you. He came around a big, empty, thousand dollar desk, and took my hand, warmly and firmly. He gripped my elbow too, and pumped my hand up and down slowly, looking into my eyes.

"Well, my God," he said. "This is really something. So you're Eric's son."

"I got to the funeral late," I said.

Something shadowed his face and he let me go. "I—uh—couldn't make it, myself." He sat back of the desk. "I was in negotiations." He picked up the phone.

"Did you want to make it?" I asked.

He lifted an eyebrow. "What kind of question is that? He was an old friend." He told the phone, "May we have some coffee in here, please?" He smiled at me. "How do you like it?"

"With lots of everything," I said.

"Breakfast roll—something?"

I nodded. "Thanks." I hadn't eaten. No money.

Niles ordered, hung up the phone, and studied me with a soft, puzzled smile. He shook his head. It was a square, dark head, the hair helmeting it in soft, regular waves, like a Roman portrait bust. It covered his ears. I thought it was a wig. It had a lot of sheen and no grey in it. His face was a delicate prize-fighter's. He said, "I can't get over how much like him you look. When I first met him."

"I'm younger," I said. "He was twenty-five."

"Right." Niles blinked and frowned. "Did—you see a lot of him? I don't remember him saying much about you."

"Never," I said, "except on TV."

"But you knew I was his friend."

"You were his lover," I said.

"Ho," Niles said softly and stood up, really surprised. But he didn't go on. The girl came in, carrying a tray with a glass coffee urn on it and brown pottery cups, and paper napkins, and a spun aluminum dome over a plate. She set it down. Niles said, "Thanks, sweetheart." She gave us a nice smile and went out. Niles sat down again and filled two mugs. "That," he said, "I don't think he would have told you. Not Eric."

"Glen Thornton told me," I said. The bowl-shaped black leather chair he had put me in was far from the desk. It was a big office. Everything was far from everything else. I got up and journeyed to the desk to spoon sugar and powdered cream substitute into my coffee. "He was at the funeral, the last one left. I wanted to know things about my father." Niles listened attentively but his suntanned hand lifted the lid off the plate where butter melted on a sugar-frosted pastry. It was sliced. I picked up a slice. Niles set the cover back. I said, "He told me more than I wanted to know."

"But you came here to follow up," Niles said.

"Because too much turned out to be not enough," I said. "Thornton was only around the edges. A long time ago, and lately." I bit the roll and chewed. It was good. So was the coffee, when I gulped a mouthful. It probably cost about a dollar a bean. "There's a lot of years to account for. Anyway"—I looked at Niles, who was working on his coffee, and not watching me; I waited until he did—"Thornton can't figure him falling out that window. And de Hooch says a lot of people could happily have pushed him."

"De Hooch?" Niles wondered.

"The man Thornton climbed into bed with after my father climbed into yours." I swallowed more coffee and asked, "Can you see Eric committing suicide?"

The outer wall of the office was glass, big metal slats outside shielding it from the sun. Niles wandered to that wall and looked out and down. He turned back with a small shudder. "No," he said. "Not Eric."

"And would some people like to kill him? Was he a bastard? Like, did he borrow money and never pay it back?"

"Actors," Niles said, "make uncertain livings."

"Even with good agents? This room says you're good."

His smile was wan. "I hadn't been Eric's agent for years."

"Why not?" I pushed the last of the butterhorn slice into my mouth and looked hungrily at the shiny plate cover. Niles lifted it again and I took another slice. "What happened?" I sat on the desk corner.

Niles regarded me over his coffee mug, doubtful, chewing his lip.

"Look," I said, "if it's too intimate or—"

"It's not that," Niles said. "I guess I find this just a little eerie. You don't know how much like him you do look. It's a kind of time-machine effect. As if he were here, young, asking me to tell him what was going to happen in his life."

"What was?" I said, and filled my mouth.

Niles sighed and sat back, frowning into the past. "Tragedy. I didn't see it that way, then. My own pain got in the way. I told myself he'd asked for it." Niles decided on more coffee and sat forward to pour it. He filled my mug at the same time, going on talking. "I'd done all right for him with small parts. Then I landed him the male lead in a low budget film opposite Joanna Payne. It was her—what?—fourth, fifth starrer. Everyone predicted a big future for Joanna. She wasn't just beautiful—she could act."

The desk was too hard on my ass, after what had happened yesterday in Venice. I sugared and creamed my coffee and took it away with me, back to the black leather chair. Niles went on talking.

"In the six, eight weeks they worked together, they"—his laugh was dry and soundless—"shall we say, became very close. It was the studio publicity department who started it, playing the usual romantic charades for the gossip magazines. Then it got a little too real, and I bitched about it. I mean, I was, let's say, pretty obsessed with Eric. He was beautiful and charming and—"

"I know the litany," I said. "Thornton recited it for me."

A corner of Niles's mouth twitched. "The charm appears not to have been passed on."

"Probably it's not genetic," I said. "And he sure as hell didn't stay around to teach me. He wanted Thornton. He wanted you."

Niles's smile was only an attempt. "Touché," he said. "Okay. So . . . I bitched about his hanging around Joanna night and day. It made me uneasy. I knew he'd been married once and fathered a child. We were good in bed together, sure. But— you can't help having doubts. I had too many. He warned me to shut up about it, but I couldn't and I didn't. The result was what you'd expect. He left me for Joanna."

"How long had it been?"

He blinked at the ceiling and let the words out slowly, unsure. "Two years? No, less than that. Say eighteen, twenty months."

"He was a stayer," I said.

"He was in for a shock." Niles's little grin said he relished the memory. "He and Joanna thought she had enough leverage in the business to dictate her leading men. They were wrong. Eric lost out on her next picture. He came back to me—not for love, for work. I wouldn't help him. I was very bruised. I told him, 'What are you bellyaching about? All you wanted her for in the first place was to live off her.' "

"Was that true?" My coffee suddenly tasted bitter.

Niles looked at me steadily. "Do you want to hate your father? Is that why you're here?"

"I want to love him." I took my mug back to the desk, set it on the tray. "But people keep making it difficult." I stirred in more sugar. "Tragedy—did you say?"

"Joanna made exactly half another picture, then she ran into a car on the freeway—head-on. It cut up her face. Plastic surgeons put it back together again, but it took months, and a lot of pain, and the nerves were never right afterward. She couldn't form expression A. For the pain they gave her morphine and she got hooked. Add to that, television had wrecked the studios. She got lost in the shuffle. Give your father this. Doctors and lawyers had taken every dime she had, but he stuck with her. He got TV work—only bit parts, but steady. He helped her kick her addiction. He set her up in a little business—antiques. But she switched over to booze. And at last he walked out. Who could blame him?"

"Not you," I said.

The phone buzzed, and one of its buttons lighted up. He pushed the button, lifted the receiver, said something into it, hung up and stood. "No," he said with a smile, "not me." He came around the desk, put an arm over my shoulder, and steered me toward the door. "I thought for a while there that I hated him. The fact was, I never stopped loving him. Eric was a disease you don't recover from."

"Did he ever love anybody?" I asked.

Niles opened the door. "He was human."

"In other words"—I looked into a hushed little paneled hall—"he didn't. Could somebody finally have murdered him for that?"

But Miss Egyptian Mummy opened the door at the other end of the hall and ushered in a white-haired giant in cowboy clothes, and Niles didn't want to answer me anyway. While the two men grabbed hands and hollered happy insults at each other, I got away.

now there's only one thing wrong with my arrangement with Catch. The nights. If I can't sleep, the house acts haunted. There's a wind that blows cold and wet and steady off the sea, and the old studs and rafters creak. Windows rattle. Once a door blew shut. And always there's someone sneaking up the staircase when there isn't. Of course, it's Sage, and this time he'll finish me. I switch on the lamp and lie shaking and sweating, with my heart slamming so hard it feels as if it will break my ribs.

Or I may get to sleep all right, then wake up later in the dark, and see Sage standing over me with the knife glinting in the dim light from the windows, and I lie paralyzed. Or I scream and try to throw myself out of the bed. I made it once, and lay shivering on the floor all night among the

Big Mac boxes and magazines till Catch came home. After that, Catch brought me sleeping pills.

But I'm scared to take them. I know how they zonk Babe out. You swallow those and for eight hours nothing, but nothing, can wake you. I wouldn't even be able to yell if Sage came. I'd never know what hit me. And that would be a lousy way to die. So, when Catch reminds me, before he takes off for work at eleven, to take my sleeping pill, I tell him I will, but I don't. I've tried to get Catch to bring me a gun to put under these pillows, but Catch is deadly afraid of guns, and he always pretends not to hear.

Anyway, now something wakes me up. My fancy watch tells me it's four fifty. It's as dark as it can get, and somebody's scrabbling at the rusty latch of the front door. It opens and closes, and somebody is climbing the stairs, and it's not the wind. "Sage!" I shout. "You son of a bitch." Nobody answers. All I hear is the slow scrape of shoes on the bare treads, and the strained sound the handrail makes. Sage wouldn't use the handrail. He'd come running up, two steps at a time. And he wouldn't wheeze.

It's the wheeze that tips me off, and I let my breath out and wipe the damp fear off my forehead. I switch on the lamp and lie back and let my heart slow down. And Doc Gallo stands in the door, with the dark at his back. His smile shows brown and broken teeth. "A failed sage," he croaks. "A successful son of a bitch." He wags his head and comes in. He walks like a sick old man, stooped, shuffling, but he's not even fifty.

He takes off his raincoat. It looks like one of

those tarps mechanics lie on to fix oil leaks under cars. His face is a river map of purple and red veins. His eyes are pale blue, bloodshot, and one of them looks off to the side. On his loose lower lip is a permanent black spot from when he passes out with cigarettes stuck there. He favors crazy headgear. This morning, it's a bandana knotted at the corners. Dirty, no-color hair straggles out from under it. He was a doctor once. Because his rich mother wanted him to be. Now that she is crazy and dying, he's a wino. His real name is Hopper.

"My last remaining skill is deserting me," he croaks. "That of eluding responsibility. Catch cornered me last night. He's worried that you're about to develop blood poisoning. I'm to inspect your wounds and give you fresh bandages." He drops the coat over the back of an old, bloated, over-stuffed chair. "Agreeable with you?"

"Have you got any sharp new patterns?" I say.

"White is always in good taste. Especially apposite for virgins. I understand they're in the bathroom in plentiful supply."

"Virgins?" I ask.

"Bandages, bandages." Doc shuffles out and down the hall toward the bathroom. "With employees like Catch, it's no wonder hospitals keep raising their rates."

I struggle out of my sweatshirt so Doc can get at the bandages. If I'm careful, my arm hardly hurts to move now. I look up at the mirror. The bandages are grey, really raunchy. Doc is a rotten doctor, but I have to give him this—he kept me shot full of dope that first week when I couldn't stand to be awake. I appreciate that my cerebral cortex is one of the models with all the extras, but the designers forgot to include an OFF switch, and when you don't want to think, you don't want to think, and Doc understood this, which very few doctors would.

I hear the old plumbing shudder. Doc is washing his hands. This is a sacrifice for him. They were filthy when he walked in. It's part of his dropout program, not washing. But all the old habits come back when he has to play medic again. Now, instead of cheap, sweet wine, the smell he brings, along with rolls of gauze and adhesive tape, is of rubbing alcohol. He's doused his hands with it after washing them. Hanging out of his dirty shirt sleeves, his hands look as if they belong to someone else.

Getting the old bandages off hurts, because they're stuck where Sage's knife went into me in that box-trap at the hospital. But Doc is pleased at the way they've shut themselves on his stitches. With fierce little scissors and tweezers, he takes the stitches out. That's fun. He uses alcohol to disinfect them. He winds the fresh gauze around me tight and expertly, and the white of it dazzles me when I look up at the mirror. I feel fine, clean, new.

Doc takes the old bandages, the unused new gauze, the tape and alcohol and the rest back to the bathroom. When he comes in again, he stands at the window and gazes out while he lights a cigarette. His hands shake. They didn't shake when they were working on me. Outside the window, there's a hint that if the West Coast is lucky, daylight may decide to show up later. Still, Doc sees something.

"Dogs." He grunts and scuffs to the chair.

"There are either twenty-eight or thirty-one," I say. "I'm not sure because they're never all out on patrol at once, and some of them look alike."

They travel the beach in a straggly pack, tongues hanging, looking around, chasing gulls off so they can nose whatever washes in with the tide. They trot past maybe a dozen times a day, first up the beach, then down the beach. They never go out on the pier. I don't know why. Maybe because they're born losers, and the pier is where the easy fish heads are.

Doc pushes soft-drink cans, paperback books, a shower of little plastic spoons and forks out of the chair, and sags into it. He asks, "Is there a leader?"

"The one that finds something to eat," I say. "He runs and they all run after him, sort of taking turns trying to grab what he's got. He swerves and stretches his neck and pops his eyes. I don't know. Maybe he thinks he'll finally get someplace alone where he can eat the thing, but I don't suppose he ever does."

"The leader." Doc sucks a tooth. "Yes."

"You probably think I'm crazy, counting dogs."

"Not at all." Through smoke, he eyes the reading-matter strewn around. Catch never reads himself, but he knows it's important to me, and he pockets anything that attracts his attention on the supermarket racks, the drugstore racks, and brings it home. I've read some pretty bad stuff to make the time go. "The printed word can pall," Doc says. "The days must be long."

"Also," I say, "the dogs are out there, I'm in here."

Doc makes a noise that is sympathetic and

gloomy. "Still, you could do worse than watch dogs. They can be very instructive. They've lived with man for aeons. And even in my lifetime, I've noticed them becoming more and more like their masters. Even to adopting man's system of ethics."

"I haven't noticed," I say.

"Ah." Doc waves a hand. "In itself, it's not much of an observation. The interest lies in the fact that these ethics, like man's, are only operative when the dog knows he's being watched."

I laugh.

But Doc wants to be taken seriously. "Which leads," he says with heavy gravity, "to the larger question, to wit—who was watching man to make him evolve as he did."

"God," I say. "Right?"

"Wrong." Doc scowls and shakes his head. "God is a creation of man. Man is not a creation of the dog."

"Okay." I shrug and the tight new bandages keep it from hurting me. "Priests," I guess, "chiefs."

"Leaders," Doc snorts. "Like your dog with the food."

"Then—" I start to say. But I stop. Because I hear Catch's Volkswagen. It clatters to a stop where he always parks it, back of the house. But it stops fast, this time, scattering gravel. And he is out of it fast, slamming the tinny door, hitting the back porch, rattling his keys in the kitchen lock. And it's too early for him—like, by two hours. I feel cold suddenly and sit very still, and don't hear what Doc is saying. Now Catch comes up the stairs at a run and is in the doorway. He looks scared, he opens his mouth to blurt something, and then sees Doc and shuts his mouth again. He relaxes, and strolls in very loose, grinning much too widely to be true. He puts on a thick Biloxi accent:

"Why, good mo'nin', doctah, suh. Hi you is?"

For some reason, there is menace in this, and Doc senses it as I do. He pushes hastily out of the chair and paws behind him for his coat, not watching what he's doing, watching Catch instead, who keeps grinning that scary grin. Doc gets the coat upside down, and a pint bottle of muscatel falls out of it and rolls on the floor to Catch's feet, who picks it up and ceremoniously hands it back. He even gives a bow. This really panics Doc. He rolls his eyes at me, ducks Catch a frightened little hitch of the shoulders, and scuttles for the door. When he's out of hearing down the stairs, I look at Catch.

"You told him to come," I say.

Catch nods bleakly, blinks, and two tears run down his face. He comes to the bed, turns back the covers, lifts me, carries me to the bathroom, sets me on the john, all without a word, just the silent crying. He turns to leave and I yelp:

"What the hell *is* it?"

Catch shuts the door. I hear him go, the same as every morning, down to get coffee. Only normally coffee would come first, before the bathroom, wouldn't it? And when I am back in bed, the routine goes off again. Catch washes me. Before we eat. The washing is good and comforting, as always. I like it very much. Only today Catch is so solemn, he won't talk, he goes over me mournfully, as if he were washing a corpse for burial. He doesn't even notice the new bandages.

"You don't make sense," I say. "What's wrong?"

Catch dries me and takes away the plastic pan, washcloth, soap, towel. He comes back, peeling his shirt, dropping his pants, sitting on the edge of the bed to get rid of his shoes, that are old and cracked and leached-out from the stuff he mops with at the hospital. Then he's with me under the covers and holding onto me hard. He's cold to the touch and he shivers. His head lies on my chest and I feel his tears cold on my skin. I touch his hair, run my hands on his shoulders and back, trying to quiet him. I lift his head by its neat little ears and look into his wet shiny eyes.

"Don't cry," I say. "Tell me what's the matter."

But instead, he burrows down under the covers and makes love to me—as they'd say in the ladies' magazines. Then he's up and kissing me hard. He's been rough before but never like this. My mouth is going to be bruised from this. At the same time, I don't want it to stop. And that is bad. I can't let myself get gone on Catch. It wouldn't be fair to him. Because when these fucking casts come off, I have to get out of here and kill Sage if I can, and nobody deserves to be mixed up in that. Catch clutches me tight. My wounds don't hurt, but I flinch as if they did, and make a sound.

"Oh, Jesus." Catch pulls back, big-eyed. "I hurt you, didn't I?" A hand comes out to touch, just barely touch, the new bandages. "Baby, I'm sorry."

I take his hand and kiss it. "It's not that bad. What's bad is how you're acting. You going to tell me now?"

The light goes out of his eyes. He gets off the bed, squats by his shirt on the floor to get cigarettes and matches out of the pocket. He stands to light the cigarette. The light from the window is sad and foggy and makes a pale grey edge along his thin, high-ass nakedness that is beautiful. He says to the window:

"You know a plainclothes pig named Sewell?"

"Oh, shit," I say.

"Because, sweetheart"—he comes back to the bed and out of habit pulls the covers up over my chest—"he know you. He's got this here drawing on this here paper. Look just like you. Except for the eyes. They too close together."

"They are too close together," I say. I feel sick to my stomach and terribly cold. I start shivering and can't stop. There's clean laundry piled on the dresser, and Catch gets me a sweatshirt and puts it on me. Catch gets into his pants and a pullover. He is grim.

"First nurse on the floor he show it to say it's you. The cute little blond boy with the broken legs that disappeared from post-op. The boy with no name and the bloody bed. All the nurses say it."

"And you?" I ask.

"Say I never seen you in my life."

"And you split early from work to come tell me."

He narrows his eyes at me, not understanding for a minute. Then he goes fast to look out the window. He trots down the hall to the bathroom where the window faces the rear. He comes in again. "He didn't follow me. Why would he follow me? What do he want with you?"

I look away. "Nothing."

Catch sits on the bed. "Why won't you tell me?"

"We've been over that. I don't want you to get

messed up in the mess I'm messed up in. Just believe me—I didn't do anything wrong." I take the cigarette from his fingers and drag on it. I hand it back. "There's nothing you can do that you're not already doing." I reach up and put my hand behind Catch's head and bring it down where I can kiss him. When the kiss is over, Catch gives a wan smile and touches my face, and says my name for the first time—softly, loving.

"Alan Tarr." He chuckles. "You awful white for tar."

"Keep joking," I say.

then blinking on the sidewalk, the flare of bright sun off the building where Niles had his office hot against my back, I shed my jacket. By reflex, I checked the pockets. There shouldn't have been anything in them. There was. A folded piece of paper. I pulled it out. It was a twenty dollar bill. I stared at it and swore. That was what Thornton was doing to the jacket before he helped me on with it. De Hooch was right about him, then, which made him right about Eric, too. But, damn it, I wasn't Eric. I had never lain still for Thornton in any sneak-away motels. I crossed the street, dodging cars, and stuck out my thumb for the long ride back across town to return the money.

But it didn't go that way. I was letting de Hooch's sneer—*like father, like son*—crowd me. Also the way everyone who knew Eric said I looked like him. I smelled casket satin, sprays of cold gladiolus, felt the seep of damp earth on my face and shuddered. I was getting schizoid or something, losing my identity. A salesman with flashy sideburns picked me up in a Galaxy so new it smelled of Detroit. He told jokes, but I didn't listen. I tried to straighten out my head. I wasn't my father, and using Thornton's money wasn't going to make me into my father. I had to stay in L.A. I couldn't stay without cash. Twenty dollars wasn't that much. I could pay it back later. I could earn it. *Selling papers in the snow,* de Hooch jeered inside my head. I ignored de Hooch, grabbed my suitcase, and jumped out at the next stoplight.

Los Angeles has a lot of shabby corners. Joanna Payne Antiques was in one of them. Past the flat-roofed grubby one-story buildings with their scabby signs, you could see, if you looked, green mountains, sky that was a good color on this particular day, and treetops in back of some places. But there was a lot of hopelessness to the grimy windows where the displays faded in the sun, the trash in the gutters, the cracked sidewalks, the fat Mexican grandmothers hobbling past with broken coasterwagons, the sick old black men sitting bony in doorways of climb-the-stairs hotels. It made me sad.

Joanna's shop was down a side street. It may have started with antiques. It had ended up with junk. The door scraped the floor as I pushed it open. The place smelled of moldy velvet. Rugs hung against the walls. Tarnished mirrors. China

was stacked on cracked marbletop tables, thick with
dust. There were two big bronze figurine lamps
with beaded shades. Spiders were living in the
shades. The place was dark after the sun-glare of
the street. It took a minute for my eyes to get used
to the gloom. Then I saw her.

She stood in a shadowy doorway at the back.
Dark paintings hung around. Her face looked like
one of them, a portrait, perfect, motionless. It
wasn't till she lifted a cigarette to her mouth that
I realised she was alive. The rest of her no one
would have bothered to paint. Cheap blond wig,
body like a stack of used luggage, dead white bare
arms and legs, blue-veined feet in old, pink, spike-
heel, open-toe shoes, nails painted pink but not
lately. The polish was chipped.

She coughed. "May I help you?"

I went toward her, edging between an Empire
sofa, its blue velvet bald in patches, and an Ali
Baba vase with a nicked rim. A grimy skylight was
over the middle of the shop. The light leaking
through hit me, and she jerked in her breath and
took a step backward.

"No," she whispered, "no."

"It's all right," I said. "I'm his son."

She laughed off her fright but shakily, and her
laugh turned into another cough. "What do you
want?"

"To talk about him. I never knew him."

"Lucky you." She turned away into the dark behind her. "All right. Come on." There was a small
sound of breaking glass. Under her breath, I heard
her say "Shit!"

I followed her. The room was crazy. Obviously,

she lived in it, but it was jammed with broken furniture, rusty bird cages, rolled-up rugs, statuary. An old melodeon grinned in a corner with yellow skull teeth. Unwashed plates, coffee cups, open tin cans, glasses and empty bottles stood on every surface. Beyond a curtain cut from faded tapestry a faucet dripped, a wornout refrigerator rattled. A pear-shape mirror with pegs in its carved frame for hanging hats was propped on the floor. It had been shrouded by a ratty Spanish shawl but the shawl had partway fallen off. Squatting to pick up pieces of the glass she'd broken, she glimpsed herself in the mirror and turned away as if she'd seen an accident.

"I don't want to be any trouble," I said.

"Hell," she said, "I want to talk about him too. Never wanted to talk about anything else." She stood up. She didn't do it well. She was older than her age. She blinked at me through cigarette smoke. "How did you find out about me? You weren't at the funeral."

I explained a little. "Toddy Niles," I said, "calls Eric a disease you never get over."

"He got over it better than some of us."

"Glen Thornton?" I asked.

"For one." She dumped the handful of glass into a bronze birdbath that was choked with cigarette butts. "Poor, weak-minded bastard. Imagine getting free of Eric for a dozen years, beautiful, blessed years"—she wagged her head—"and then, the minute he walks in your door again, handing him two thousand bucks. Because he says he needs it, he's down on his luck. Two thousand smackers."

She dropped onto a couch that was butt-sprung

at the end where she obviously always sat. Her hand went out for a bottle. Mechanically. The cigarette hung in a corner of her mouth. It looked as if it was sticking out of a mask. Her face was like that, a mask. And if she let the rest of herself go, she must have spent hours on the mask—or maybe she didn't have to, maybe the surgeons had done it all. You've never seen a woman's face as beautiful. But a young woman's, and perfect as porcelain, glazed-looking. And without life, a dead face, even though the eyes moved, the mouth moved, and words came out—words like "smackers." Who said that anymore?

I told her, "You haven't got it quite right. Eric made love to him. And he paid for it. Five hundred dollars a time."

"And cheap at half the price," she said, and started to cough. This time she couldn't stop. She set the wine bottle down, clutched her throat, bent forward. Her whole body jerked. The sounds ripped out of her, deep and deadly. But people twist their faces up when they cough. Not her. It was creepy, like watching a big puppet. It took time, but it did end. The cigarette still stuck to her pink lipstick. Her hand went down beside the couch and came up with tissues, and she very carefully blotted tears off her face. I wondered how she felt them. "Sit down," she said. "I'd offer you some of this, but you look a little young." She slopped red wine into a flower-painted teacup.

"How did you learn about the Thornton affair?" I lifted a limp stack of old *Photoplay* magazines out of a Roman campaign chair, and sat down. "Is Thornton a friend of yours?"

"Never laid eyes on the man." She stretched for

the birdbath to stub out her cigarette. "Jack de Hooch came here hunting for Eric, when he found out what was going on."

"Why here? I thought you and Eric broke up."

"Joanna Payne Antiques"—she sparked another cigarette with a lipstick-shape lighter, and her laugh was cheerless—"was Eric's—what word do I want?—refuge?" She tasted the wine. "When there was no place else out of the rain, he'd come here. Not *here* at first—I had a shop in Beverly Hills, first."

"What happened to that?"

"You think I drank it up, right? Wrong, Baby. Look—" She got to her feet. "I think I've changed my mind. Your father was a nice man, a beautiful man, a man I loved. Let's let it go at that, huh, sweetheart?"

"Let's not," I said. "Please. I want to know about him. He was my father. What happened to your shop?"

Something twitched in the porcelain face. The effect was scary. Maybe it pained her, because she shut her eyes for a second. Then she did something with her mouth that may have been meant for a smile. She shrugged and sat down again. "Okay," she sighed. "I could never go against him. I can't go against you, either. God, but you do look like him." She tilted her head, staring. The stare looked wistful and sex-hungry.

"I don't have his charm," I said. "What happened to your shop?"

"Each time Eric came and 'helped me out,' he left behind a cash-drawer full of empty."

"I thought he set you up in business."

"He did." She nodded. "But over the years, he

got it all back. Not meaning to. It was just the way his luck ran. He couldn't help it."

"Yeah." I glanced around the place. Cobweb hammocks, sleep-filled with dust, hung in the dark, high corners. "And you call Thornton weak-minded."

"I didn't say I wasn't. I was." She got up again. "Listen, I think there's some tomato juice in the cupboard. I'll put an ice-cube in it."

"Don't worry about me," I said, but she went on out through the tapestry curtain anyway and rattled around, running water, prying out ice-cubes, dropping things. Over the noise, she went on talking. "He never quite wiped me out, after all. I'm still here. There's still a living in it."

"He won't be back," I said. "That should make it easier from now on."

"That won't make it easier, no."

"What happened when Jack de Hooch came in? Was Eric here?"

She returned and handed me a finger-smeared glass with tomato juice and ice, and told me what I expected she was going to tell me. "He was here, and de Hooch said if he didn't keep away from Glen Thornton, he'd kill him. He, de Hooch, would kill Eric, that is." She jerked the beautiful head in the frazzled wig at the door opening. "Right out there in the shop, standing there with his raincoat dripping, making a puddle on the floor, and with a gun in his hand."

"Wow," I said. "How did Eric take it?"

She drank what was left in her teacup and blinked at me over the rim. "Are you brave?" she asked. "You strike me as being brave."

"I'm a lion," I said. "I don't know."

"You are," she said as if she knew. "I was wondering what was so different about you from him. And that's what it is. You must have got it from your mother. You sure as hell didn't get it from Eric. Eric was not brave." She filled the painted cup again and coughed a sour laugh that sounded like dice in a bar-room shaker. "He ran back into this room with de Hooch after him, and it was me who pulled de Hooch by the arm and shoved him out the front door. Eric was down behind this couch. He wouldn't come out for a long, long time. You know why? He didn't want me to see."

"See what?"

"He'd pissed himself," she said.

She was really cheering me up. I wanted to leave, but I stayed. "Maybe he didn't keep away from Thornton," I said, "and de Hooch kept his word and killed him."

Shock made her jerk, and wine spilled red down the pink front of her dress. Not that it mattered. It had spilled there before. "No one killed him," she said. "He committed suicide."

I told her Thornton's theory about actors with unreleased pictures.

"It's good psychology. There's just one little flaw in it." She dabbed at the dribbled wine with tissues. "He didn't wait, did he? He killed himself. That was the coroner's verdict."

"Was he sick?" I said. "Cancer or something?"

"Not according to the autopsy." She flipped the wadded tissues at the birdbath and dragged grimly on her cigarette. "No. I suppose his new boyfriend found out the heel he was and left. And, unlikely as it may seem, Eric this time had stepped into the trap. Eric had fallen in love. He wouldn't be used to someone walking out on him. He wouldn't know how to handle it. In his life, he was the one who did the walking out."

"Starting with me," I said.

"I'll tell you this much," she said, "there was definitely no goodlooking young man in widow's weeds at that funeral. They were all old, familiar faces."

"De Hooch told me a lot of people would have liked to kill him." I drank tomato juice and wiped my mouth with the back of my hand. "Would that include you?"

Her eyes narrowed, and for a second I thought she was going to jump me, claws out. It didn't happen. Instead, she laughed. It was one of the saddest sounds I ever heard. "If I were going to kill Eric, I wouldn't have waited. I'd have done it after the accident."

"But he stuck by you after that—didn't he?"

"He stuck by me—when he found out I was going to live. But not on the freeway. He wiped his fingerprints off the steeringwheel and left me there to die."

I felt sick. Sicker. "He was with you?"

"He was driving. It was my car, but he was driving." She drained the cup of wine and filled it again. "He explained afterward that it would only have wrecked his career, and what good would that do? How could he have helped me then?" She sighed. A crumb of tobacco stuck to the rim of the cup. She pinched it off. "Well, it wasn't his fault. That damn Pasadena freeway is a nightmare. Ought to be condemned. So . . . I let it stand like that. You're the first person I've ever told." She looked at me with tears in her eyes. "Why not? It doesn't matter now. Nothing matters now."

"He was a creep," I said.

"He wasn't a hero," she said. "He was an actor."

Maybe I was more disgusted with her than with him. Maybe only because she was there. "You'd forgive him anything, wouldn't you? You and Thornton and Niles. I don't understand it."

"You never knew him," she said gently. "Sometimes he talked about you. He was proud of having a son. He wondered what you were growing up like."

"He could have come and found out."

"He was afraid of your mother—what's her name?"

"Babe." I grinned. "Yeah—there's one who wouldn't have had him back. She knew what he was."

But I wondered if I was right. I wondered if, at some point, he'd stood in the trailer door, handsome, smiling, charming as everybody kept saying he was, Babe wouldn't have taken him back, kept him around for as long as he'd stay. Thinking about it, about the fact that Eric cared for me, wondered about me, gave me a weird feeling in my stomach, half queasy and half weepy with happiness. I loved the son of a bitch with absolutely no reason to. If he ever had come back, if I had ever gotten to know him, I'd really be messed up. As Joanna said, *lucky you*. Only I didn't feel lucky. I felt left out.

Joanna got off the couch and worked her way into the darkness on the far side of the room. She began shifting junk around. She had been talking but I hadn't been listening. I caught the end of a sentence. "—not with a gun. If he was murdered, somebody pushed him out a window. I made a costume picture once." She grunted with the effort of whatever she was doing. "In historical times, it was popular to kill people that way. You know what they call it? Defenestration. Who'd connect that with somebody dying? I mean, it's such a pansy word."

She really had a vocabulary. The last thing she'd read must have been a script by James M. Cain. "Pansy was what he was," I said.

She said, "It's true—you don't have his charm."

"But I'm brave," I said. "Did you always know he was a fag?"

"Oh, yes, I knew it. Did it matter?"

That shook me. "It's supposed to."

"You're very young," she said.

"So they tell me. Who did he leave you for?"

"Oh, God, who remembers their names? There were so many of them. Pat and Mike, and Tom and Dick—"

"And Bruce," I said. "Jesus."

"But when he wanted stability, he came back to me." She brought cardboard cartons stacked on top of each other and dumped them on the couch. Dust flew like in the first reel of *The Grapes of Wrath*. She had another coughing fit. When it was over, she wiped her eyes and blew her nose, and gave that harsh, sad laugh of hers. "Stability! Who the hell am I kidding? Money, love—you name it. He knew if I had it, it was his. Face it. I could care less what man he'd been using, or how, or why.

He was back. That was all that mattered." She tried to work the smile again and failed. She touched my hair, looking down at me, wistful-eyed. "It's what's called love. You don't act much like him, but you have got his looks. I hope for your sake you've got his heart too. Cold stone. It'll save you a lot of grief."

"It earned him enough to kill him," I said, and nodded at the cartons. "What's all this?"

"His estate." She left off smoothing my hair, and flapped open the top carton. She lifted out a jacket that had been in style last year. "Actors like Eric may not have much but clothes they have to have. I was going to take them to the thrift shop around the corner. I'm glad now I didn't. They'll fit you."

"How did you get them? You don't mean he kept them here. He had an apartment."

"The County impounded them, but what the hell use were they to them? When I claimed I was his common-law wife—which I did, loud and shrill, thinking like a fool there might be some money, which there wasn't—they couldn't wait to give me the clothes."

"Had he promised you money?" I said.

"It was stupid of me to believe him." She tilted wine into the teacup again. "No. What I got was what I'd always figured to get—his clothes to cry into a night or two, and then stuff into a closet." She gulped the wine.

"I can't take them." I needed a suit to replace the one Babe would kill me for losing in the canal, but it was going to be awkward getting one without getting all. "I don't have transportation. I don't have anyplace to stay."

She jumped at that. "Stay here." She headed for the tapestry curtain again. "There's more room than you'd believe. Look." She held the curtain back.

I went and looked. I got a fast impression of a grease-yellowed stove piled with crusty frying pans, a ceiling vent hung with ragged curtains of black cobweb, soup bowls sprouting mold, and I didn't look at the kitchen anymore. Beyond the kitchen loomed a long storage room—broken crystal chandeliers, upended walnut table tops, dirty cutglass wrapped in moth-eaten sarapes, a harp without strings, cabinets with bellied glass doors.

"That's a good bed, very comfortable."

I could see it rearing up under a high, grimy window in a far corner, carving and more carving, with a matching chest of drawers beside it, topped by a dust-fogged mirror. There wasn't another bed. I guessed she and Eric wouldn't have wanted two—or at least she wouldn't. One thing—they wouldn't have been crowded. The period was General Grant. The bed could have slept Grant *and* the Army of the Tennessee.

"Thanks," I said, "but I guess I'll head home."

"You won't. You're looking for answers."

"To who killed him," I said, "and why."

She let the curtain fall and turned. "He did it himself. I told you why. He was infatuated with some boy. That much I know for a fact." She walked off.

I said, "How much money did he owe you?"

She turned. "I don't know any numbers that large."

"How badly do you need it? Are you really all

right? This place doesn't exactly give that impression. What would happen to you if you lost it?"

She didn't answer. She poured wine. Shakily.

I asked, "Did you go to his place to collect? Did he laugh at you? Did you push him out the window?"

Her mouth twitched. She wanted to scream at me, but she didn't. It was interesting to watch. Niles was right. She could act. She dropped onto the couch again. Her voice was easy, amused, taunting. "As a detective, you're dreadful, child. Much too crude. You ought to study those old Falcon pictures with George Sanders. Now there was a smoothie."

I loved her slang but not much else about her. "How did you know he was hung up on this boy?"

She shrugged and tossed off the wine. "He came by for something he'd left here—I forget what. He told me."

"He had real tact," I said.

Her look was pitying. "You don't understand."

"Did he tell you the boy's name?" Negative. "Did you see the boy when you went to Eric's apartment?"

"I never went there—not till he was dead." She wobbled to her feet. Awkwardly. The teacup fell off the arm of the couch. It didn't break. There were two thicknesses of dusty throw-rug at her feet. The cup lay there bleeding. "Give up," she told me. "Or, if you must play Bogart, play it with somebody else. Sean Raftery. If anyone wanted to kill Eric, it was Sean. No, don't ask." She sulked. "Leave me alone. Go on." She waved a limp, weary, disgusted hand. "Nosey little squirt, anyway. Scram, will you? Scram."

I scrammed, if that was the correct past tense. But before I reached the gritty street-corner, I heard her calling me. I turned. She was in the shop doorway, beckoning me back. "You didn't have any lunch."

"I'm not hungry," I called. And I wasn't.

The motel was in a fold of the brushy green hills that hedge Cahuenga pass, between Hollywood and the San Fernando Valley. The glare of noon did the building no favors. It wasn't old, but the paint was flaking off it. Rafter ends were warped. So were the second story decks that ran past numbered plywood doors. Facing the same kind of doors below, cars were parked on the bias on weedy asphalt. The doors were all closed. The cars had their backs to a tile swimming-pool, cracked down one side and across its bottom, probably by some earthquake. The crack had been cemented shut. The blue water looked inviting. I'd hitch-hiked up from Hollywood Boulevard, where a bus had dropped me, and I was sweaty.

At the far end of the pool, out of the sun and backed by a clump of banana trees, three men without shirts sat on aluminum and webbing chairs and played cards at a metal table. I had seen them a hundred times on television—so had everybody. One was fat, half bald, and his skin was red and peeling. The second was brown and leathery, with a pushed-in face. The third was small and wiry, with tightly crimped red hair. His skin was freckled. None of them was young. I walked along to where they were playing and watched for a minute. I didn't recognize the game. The leathery one saw my suitcase and pointed.

"Office is over there, at the front."

"There's no one in it," I said. "Anyway, I don't want to stay. I'm looking for a man who lives here."

The other two had been studying their cards. Now they looked at me. This meant the little red-haired one had to turn. When he saw me, he stood up and his chair went over with a frail clatter on the flagging.

"Your name is Tarr," he said.

"Right. Alan. Are you Sean Raftery?"

"What do you want?"

The next action on one of the TV shows you'd see Raftery in would have been for me to look significantly at the other two men and back to Raftery, and say, in a flat, quiet voice, "Is there someplace private we can talk?" And that is what I did.

Raftery knew what the script called for. He tightened his face. "What about?"

"My father. He's dead. You knew that."

"Killed himself. It was on the TV News." Raftery righted his chair. "Look, kid, I'm sorry for you." He sat down. "But it's nothing to me. He was no friend of mine." He picked up his cards.

"I don't think he killed himself," I said. "I think somebody murdered him. And I'm told that if anybody would want to do that, it would be you."

"Oh-oh," the fat man said, and Raftery stood up and took my elbow in hard, bony fingers, and steered me fast along the edge of the pool, between two dusty ten-year-old cars, and through one of the numbered doors. There was a bed with a fitted cover, a couch, a chair, a coffee table, lamps, standard motel stuff. A portable color TV, an air conditioner humming in a window. Raftery shut the door with his foot, and gave me a shove so that I hit the couch sitting.

"Now what is this? The police said he killed himself. The Coroner's jury said he killed himself. What are you trying to do?"

"I've been backtracking through his life," I said. "See, I never knew him. But all I've heard from people who did"—a mimeographed shooting script lay open on the coffee table, blue paper covers, brass brads; I flipped the pages—"says he wasn't the type to kill himself. For openers, he was a coward. Somebody did it to him. And there were several people with reasons."

"And what's supposed to be mine?" Raftery took the script out of my hands and tossed it onto the bed.

"I don't know. That's what I came to find out."

Raftery stared at me. Then he laughed. It was a laugh for cameras, for microphones. It didn't convince me. Raftery turned away chuckling, wagging his head, and went into a stingy kitchenette, where he popped open cans. He came back, grinning, and handed a can to me. It was beer, and I was thirsty, and afraid to cross the man, so I tasted it. It was yeasty and bitter, but I liked it. I wished someone else had given it to me.

"All right." Raftery dropped onto the bed, put

his feet up, stretched out with his head and shoulders propped on throw pillows. "Who told you I'd be the most likely one to murder your old man?"

"I'd rather not say."

"Uh-huh. Okay. What the hell. It could have been a lot of different people, actors, grips, secretaries—who knows? I was pissed off, and I didn't keep it to myself. If I'd known he was going to die, I would have." He crossed his ankles and drank from his beer can. "Why didn't your informant tell you the story?"

"She was bored with my questions."

He snorted. "I can see how that might happen."

"What was the story?"

"Let me show you something." He got up, opened a closet, crouched, and dug around in the dark. When he backed out, hanging clothes brushed his hair so it stood up ragged. He smoothed it down with one hand. The other hand held a script, thicker than the blue one. When he dropped it on the table in front of me, it made a solid thud. "Look at that. Look at what's written on that."

The cover was yellow. There was writing in black felt pen in the top right-hand corner. *Mr. Sean Raftery—Sec. of State.* I raised my eyebrows. "Secretary of State?"

"It's the character in the picture—the part your father played. I can understand your not knowing. It hasn't been released yet."

"The title is right," I said. "I read it in *Variety,* in the piece about his dying, his funeral." I frowned at Raftery. "What does this mean—the handwriting?"

"It means the part was supposed to be mine. My agent closed the deal. Verbally. The producers sent me the script. Shooting was supposed to start in ten days. I was getting the lines, my agent was supposedly getting the contract, when he telephoned me the deal was off."

I leafed over the script. The Secretary of State's lines were underlined in red pencil. There were a lot of them. "Looks like a good part," I said.

Raftery nodded glumly. "You're damn right. In and out, all through the screenplay. Best I had in years." His laugh was wry. "To be honest—best I ever had. When I saw how big it was, it scared me. I couldn't believe my luck. Still, it figured. Did you read the novel? Best seller."

"My book club membership ran out."

"Yeah? Well, about a million people did read it, I guess. And when they came to cast the picture, they wanted actors that looked the way the characters were described in the book. The Secretary of State was a little, wiry, redheaded guy about forty-five, right? So I was ideal for it, wasn't I?"

"My father didn't have red hair," I said.

"In the picture he did," Raftery said. "Hell, dying his hair was nothing compared to what else—" He broke off, shook his head, drank from the beer can, set it down on the lamp stand, shook a cigarette from a pack on the stand, and lit it. "Look," he said through the smoke, "you don't want to hear this. I mean—he was your father."

"How did he get the part when you already had it?"

Raftery sighed and sat up, swung his feet to the wall to wall carpet, and leaned forward, elbows resting on his knees, hands hanging. He frowned and worked his mouth, worried, eyeing me. "How—uh—how, well, sophisticated are you, kid?"

"If you mean," I said, "do I know he was queer—yes, I know he was queer."

Raftery jerked out a little laugh like a terrier's bark. At himself. "Yeah, it figures. Kids today." He got his beer can again, lifted it to his mouth, and before he drank said, "Okay, you know. So . . . that's the story. All there is to it." He drank, head back, Adam's apple jerking.

"I'm not that sophisticated," I said. "What are you trying to say?"

"It started with agents." Raftery lay back again, and talked to the ceiling. "There's small agents and big agents. If you're a bit player you've usually got a small agent. He does what he can for you. If you get the right parts, you build an image, a public that wants to see more of you. And you may still be a bit player, but you find a big agent, who gets you more work, who gets you more money. Anyhow, I've got a small agent."

"My father wasn't any more famous than you."

"Less. But there's a big agent in this town who can really make things happen. And once upon a time, a long time ago, probably before you were born, this big agent was a little agent, starving along with the rest of us. In those not-so-good-old-days, this agent was your father's agent."

Trying to be casual, I tilted my beer can too high, drinking. Beer ran down my chin. I wiped it with my hand and wiped the hand on my Levi's and said, "Toddy Niles."

Raftery peered at me from the pillows. "You know this story?"

"I talked to Niles this morning. But only ancient history. Not current events. He said he hadn't been my father's agent for a long time."

"He lied to you. Did he tell you that when they were boys together, they were girls together?"

"Lovers." Something in the way he put it made me want to change the wording. "He didn't need to tell me. Someone else already had."

"What are you doing, writing his biography?"

I shook my head. "It would read too monotonous."

"Then you're wasting your time." He twisted out his cigarette in a glass ashtray that had the name of the motel chain in its bottom. "The police took care of the case. There's no need for you to play private eye."

"I'm not. Not really." I shrugged. "Suddenly, when he was dead, I just wanted to know about him. Maybe I discovered I'd missed him all this time."

"You like what you've learned?"

"No. But if somebody killed him, they'd be a lot worse than he was. He never murdered anybody."

"Neither did I." Raftery emptied his beer down his stringy throat and went back to the kitchenette for another. "You ready yet?"

"I've still got half a can," I said. I also had a small buzz on. Raftery leaned on the counter that separated the kitchenette from the main room. It was decorated with fake planters of fake trailing vines and ferns. I said to him, "But you told people that you'd like to kill him. Over this shafting he gave you about the part."

"True." Raftery gestured. "It's an expression. 'I could kill that son of a bitch.' You know? Everybody says it sometimes—right?" He smiled hopefully.

I didn't smile back. "Sometimes they mean it," I said. "So he got Toddy Niles to shoulder your agent and you out of the picture by sleeping with Niles again?"

"You're halfway there." Raftery worked the slat blinds over the air conditioner and stared out up a slope where ragged ivy geranium tried to get a grip on the yellow bulldozed hillside. "Niles at that time was sleeping with Frenchy Beautran, who cast this picture."

"Did my father know that?"

"The word was around. In this business you listen to every rumor. You believe maybe one tenth of them, but you sure as hell don't forget any."

"Okay." I picked up the suitcase and stood. "I can see why you're upset."

Raftery snorted. "Yeah. First time in my life I regretted liking broads. It's a big picture. Could have made a lot of difference to me."

"Well, there's one consolation." I pulled open the flimsy door. "It can't help him. Not now."

Raftery turned from the window. "Just one thing. When he died, I was on location with a TV special. Rodeos. In Wyoming. I didn't push him out that window."

"Not unless they gave you a very fast horse," I said, and walked out into the sun.

96

Niles's house was in Palos Verdes, maybe thirty miles from his office, where Miss Miracle of the Embalmers Art told me he'd gone home for the afternoon because he had scripts to read and didn't want to be interrupted. I wanted to interrupt him, so I used Thornton's money to take a cab. Buses, trains, and planes didn't go that way. The place hung lonely—naked cement beams and plate glass, flat roof covered with white rocks—on a cliff between hard blue sky and hard blue ocean.

A copy of a 1933 Auburn was parked in front, but no one came when I pressed a doorbell, so I turned a grapefruit-size brass knob in the center of a redwood slab door, the door opened, and I walked into a long, low-ceilinged room where it was hard to see the furniture because of the day-glare through the glass wall that faced the sea. I jarred a table and a big Tiffany lamp on it tottered. I kept it from falling, and moved on.

The low king size bed had been busy, and no one had made it up afterward. On its far side, white pleated drapes had been drawn back the width of one glass wall panel, and the panel stood open. Outside was a raw cement deck and a raw cement swimmingpool. Why this looked expensive I didn't know—something to do with a magazine I used to look at in libraries: *Japan Architect*, I guess. Niles lay beside the pool on a mat cased in flowered fabric. He was propped on an elbow. Except for sunglasses, he was naked. Scripts were stacked beside him, sure enough, and one lay open on the mat. A drink was in his hand, tall, pale, with a sprig of mint.

But he wasn't reading or drinking. He was watching a naked young man do porpoise dives in the pool, splashing. His ass looked dead white in the sun, because the rest of him was tanned very dark. Niles laughed words at him, but I couldn't decipher them over the water noises. I stepped out on the deck, and Niles set the glass down to keep from dropping it. He lost his smile, and sat up. But not fast. He pushed the shades up on his fringed forehead. He didn't look guilty. Startled was how he looked.

"Where did you come from?"

"The door was open," I said. "This is a hard place to find. Taxi driver had to ask in a filling-station." I looked at the pool where the young man was treading water now, plastering back long hair behind his ears, and staring. It gave me an idea. "Can I swim too?"

Niles relaxed and grinned. Like an alligator. "If I can watch."

The grin shook me a little, but I wanted Niles disarmed, and I guessed what would disarm some-body like Niles would be to see a young dude na-ked, especially since I was a duplicate of my father when he was young. "It's your pool." I shrugged, stripped, and fell into the water. "They're your eyes."

"Thanks," Niles said. "Alan Tarr, Tombstone Smith."

Smith and I nodded to each other with small toothy smiles like dogs. "How long can you stay under?" Smith asked me.

"Long enough to race you." Smith was bigger, and should have had deeper lungs. Niles was wearing a skin-diver watch. "Time us," I said, and he nodded.

I won. Both times. Probably because the pool was cramped for Smith's long arms and legs, and I could turn in it like a minnow. Niles went someplace and brought back a beachball, and got into the water too, and we skidded the ball around, batted it around, wrestled it around. Our bodies brushed together as often as Niles could manage it. It obviously gave him pleasure, and Tombstone didn't seem to mind it, but when the two of them started forgetting the ball entirely, in favor of each other, I climbed out of the pool, found a bathroom, and took a long shower.

When I came out, Tombstone was sprawled face down on sheets even more rumpled than when I'd seen the bed first. His face was turned sideways against the pillows, mouth slightly parted. He breathed slow, deep in sleep. His cowboy hair was going to need a lot of combing later, but that didn't spoil the effect. I stood there with my jaw hanging and stared at him. The character was really beautiful. For maybe ten whole seconds, I understood Niles wanting to get it on with him. I didn't like understanding that, and I went for my Levi's, and then to find Niles. He was in the kitchen, still naked, whistling between his teeth, a contented fag.

I leaned in the doorway. "No wonder everybody in this town knows everybody's business."

Niles glanced at me with a little frown, but he didn't stop what he was doing, peeling and slicing avocados. "Some people there's no point in keeping some secrets from," he said. "Or even trying."

"Why me? I'm dangerous," I said. "Grr."

"This morning, I believed that." With a knife, he scraped the avocado chunks off the cutting board into a wooden chopping bowl. "You came on very butch." He began mashing the avocados with a steel fork. "The way you looked at my receptionist saddened me." He cut a lemon and squeezed half of it over the mash. "That's why I took the afternoon off." He picked lemon seeds out of the bowl, flicked them into the sink, licked his fingers. "And picked up Tombstone on my way home."

"He doesn't look like a substitute," I said. "He looks like the original. His name should be Adam."

"As a matter of fact"—Niles rummaged in a cupboard—"it isn't Tombstone."

"You surprise me," I said.

Niles found what he wanted, a bottle of Jalapeña sauce. "It's Hurlbut Price Webster, the third." He uncapped the jar and spooned some of the watery green contents into the wooden bowl and began blending it in with the fork. "A very old and distinguished San Marino family. Corporation law. Loaded with money. But he wants to be a cowboy star. If his analyst can get him over his fear of horses, he may make it."

"He'll make it," I told Niles's pretty welterweight profile. "He's got you. And you can get anybody anything in motion pictures."

"Fantasy." Niles scooped up some of the mixture in the bowl on a finger and licked the finger and approved what he tasted. He nodded at the bowl. "Guacamole," he said. "Try some?"

"I can wait," I said. "It wasn't fantasy when you did it for Eric in that last film. When you made him Secretary of State."

Niles had turned the water on at the sink. The disposal mechanism chuckled as if it enjoyed the lemon seeds. Niles stood very still, holding his hands under the water that came out of a swing tap with a soft fizzing sound, aerated, probably softened. I went on:

"You lied to me in your office when you said you hadn't been his agent for a long time. You were his first agent, but you were also his last, his very last."

"You've been listening to gossip." Niles turned off the water and dried his hands on a towel printed with yellow daisies to match the wallpaper. His smile was too bright. "You don't want to believe everything you hear."

"I don't want to, but Sean Raftery made me believe this." I told Niles why, about the script, and so on.

"Ho." Niles blinked at me with a small frown, teeth nibbling his lower lip. "You meant that about being dangerous, didn't you?" He took down a glass like his own, rattled half-circles of ice from a refrigerator big enough to entertain in, dropped the ice into a glass and brought out a bottle. "Bitter orange?"

"I wish," I said loudly, "that everybody would stop being so goddam nice to me."

Niles shut the refrigerator door. "They will—but not for quite a while. Not till you're old and ugly."

"I wish you hadn't lied to me." I watched him open the bottle. "I wish I could like somebody that knew him."

Niles gave me the glass to hold. "You haven't tried me yet." He poured from the bottle into the glass. "I'll send Tombstone home."

"You mistake my meaning," I said.

Niles sighed. "I was afraid I had." He ripped open a big bag of tostado chips and poured from it into another wooden bowl, and picked up both bowls, and walked out, saying over his shoulder, "Will you bring my drink?"

I brought it, and watched him set the bowls on a coffee table in front of a long couch that faced the glass wall that looked at the sea. Whitecaps drew chalk lines on the sea, that erased themselves and drew themselves again, and erased themselves. Niles dropped onto the couch and looked up at me with his hand out. I gave him his drink.

"Did you kill him?" I said.

Maybe he in fact had been a fighter. For a second, he looked mean enough. "You know," he said, "you're not very big, and you don't look very strong. Suppose I had killed him and I thought you knew it. Don't you suppose I'd kill you too?"

"Not with your secretary knowing you were here and I was coming here." I jerked my head at the bedroom. "And not with a witness. If you didn't kill Eric, why did you lie to me?"

He smiled. "There could be a lot of reasons."

"I'll settle for the real one," I said. "Maybe I know enough about him now to guess it. Stop me when I go wrong. He came to see you. Surprise! He handed you a line about how he'd always loved you, nobody else had meant anything, couldn't you start over together."

"Too crude." Niles sipped his gin and tonic. "You forget he was an actor, and a damn good one."

"Okay," I said. "He cried or something, right?"

"He laughed," Niles said, "but in a desolate way, much more moving than tears. Ah—the details don't matter." He got up and took his drink to the plate glass. "Hell, he didn't have to do anything, say anything. I was his. I always had been his."

"You were lovers with a man called Beautran," I said. "All Eric wanted was for you to get Beautran to cast him in that picture. He was just using you."

Niles's answer blurred off the glass. "Right."

"And you lost Beautran?"

"Once filming started, I told him goodbye. Eric was what I wanted, what I'd always wanted."

"And then Eric walked out on you for some boy?"

Niles turned. "You know all there is to know."

"And you weren't hurt enough to kill him for that?"

Niles scooped guacamole onto a chip and came up with a smile and a shrug. "I found a boy of my own."

"Tombstone," I said. "But you were ready to shake him off for me a couple of minutes ago."

Niles chewed and swallowed. "I said you were very like Eric."

"And you never learn," I said.

Four men sat in a room that had brown woodwork, grimy white walls, and too many file cabinets. The men worked at desks with telephones, typewriters, plastic cups, papers. Tired sunlight slanted across them from big windows. The man nearest the door, who had loosened a nothing necktie on a wilted white collar, and who needed a shave and probably a bath, looked at me with eyes that bulged under thick lids and were blood-shot.

"What do you need?" He underlined the you wearily.

"They told me downstairs to see Lieutenant Sewell."

"Over here," Sewell said. He was dialing a phone with the rubber end of a pencil. He stopped and dropped the receiver in place and pushed back a creaky swivel chair. He looked as if he would play more football if anyone asked him, but he was past forty, and his chest was sagging, and he had the beginnings of a belly. No one was going to ask him. Across his cheekbones was a fine network of little red veins, and he kept his hair clipped close, but you could see that it was thinning. He shook my hand.

"I'm Alan Tarr. You were in charge of, like, my father's case? Eric Tarr? The actor?"

"Sit down." Sewell nodded at a hard yellow oak chair. I sat, and it hurt, and I remembered Piper. Sewell said, "What's on your mind?"

"Did he kill himself?"

Sewell sighed and dug a cigarette from a dam-aged pack on the desk. It already had a filter, but he stuck it into a small white mouthpiece. "It's what's called an equivocal suicide. Three thousand people in Los Angeles try suicide every year. Six hundred of them make it. Of that six hundred, about ten percent get tagged equivocal."

"Meaning you don't know for sure?"

"Meaning, it could have been an accident." He pawed among papers and found a tattered matchbook, and lit the cigarette. "He didn't leave a note. Not that that's conclusive. Only about a third of them leave notes."

"Do three thousand people fall out windows?"

He twitched a smile. It didn't have humor in it. "Almost none. But in the interests of accuracy, it wasn't a window. It was a balcony."

"I only read about it in *Variety*," I said. "They called it a window."

"Then you never saw his apartment?"

"I never saw him. Not since I was a baby. I came here for his funeral."

Sewell shook his head. "You weren't there."

"I got there too late. Why were you there?"

He waited a second, then shrugged. "Routine."

"I don't think so," I said. "I don't think anyone has time to go to that many funerals. You wanted to see who came, because you don't think he jumped. Or fell, either. You think somebody pushed him."

Sewell's smile widened by a centimeter. "I don't know what to think, and that makes me uneasy." The phone rang. He picked it up and said monosyllables into it and hung it up again. "When I've got time to be uneasy." A stack of manila folders was at his elbow. He shuffled the stack and opened a folder. A photo lay on top inside, an eight-by-ten glossy. A woman in a torn dress sprawled on dirty linoleum. Something terrible had happened to her. I shut my eyes. When I opened them, Sewell had turned the photo over, and was making a note in pencil on a form. "But I hardly ever have time." He shut the folder and laid it on top of the stack. "As you suggest."

"I think somebody pushed him," I said.

Sewell nodded. "That's not uncommon. Families have that reaction to suicide. They feel guilty when a loved one takes his own life. They look for someone else to blame."

"He wasn't my loved one," I said. "I wasn't his."

"But you came to his funeral—or you wanted to."

"Okay," I said. "We loved each other, but neither one of us knew it. I didn't know I gave a damn about him till he was dead. I didn't know he gave a damn about me till someone I never saw before told me. Today."

Sewell let his smile come back, as if it were a dog trained to bite only on command. "So, I'm right, no?" I started to argue but the phone rang and Sewell picked up the receiver. This time he put it back after listening only a few seconds. He stood up, said, "Excuse me," and left the room.

I sat and listened to the chatter of teletype machines next door, like the spring-equipped jaws of maybe twenty of those china skulls you see in joke stores. Someplace farther off, a woman's voice went on and on, angry and protesting. A map of Hollywood hung above the file cabinets back of Sewell's desk. The map was faded and full of pinholes. In its frame, pins with colored heads waited for trouble. The phone rang on the desk of the weary man by the door, and he picked it up wearily, and spoke wearily into it. A muscular girl in uniform came in and leaned across me to drop papers into a plastic tray on Sewell's desk. I looked out the window. Shaggy silhouettes of old eucalyptus trees sheltering a sanitarium across the street moved a little in a slow breeze against a sky that for bad taste would have disgusted a sentimental little old lady painter of sunsets.

Sewell came back. "Sorry to keep you waiting." A striped paper cup was in each of his hands. He put one cup on the desk corner for me, and sat down with his own. "It's from a machine, and it's not very good, but it's what there is," he said.

"Thanks." I tried it. It tasted something like Coke and something like cold. "Explain to me," I said. "He'd just finished the best role he'd had in years, in a big motion picture. He'd been well paid. The picture isn't out yet. He'd want to see it. Also, it would boost his career. Why would somebody who'd been trying for a lifetime and finally made it kill himself?"

"This will surprise you, but it's a pattern we look for. Any abrupt change in the life-style. Sudden success can be as upsetting to a man as sudden failure. Especially a middle-aged man."

"You've been into the literature," I said.

Sewell nodded, shutting his eyes, opening them. "This is a job with a lot of questions. I like all the answers I can get."

"Try these," I said. "First, a woman named Joanna Payne, who was climbing in pictures before my father smashed up her car and her face in a freeway crash. He sponged off her for years, promising to pay her back some day when he made it. He made it—and she's down as far as she can get, and he didn't give her a dime. Why couldn't she have pushed him off that balcony?"

Sewell cocked an eyebrow, drank from his cup, waited.

"And a man named de Hooch," I said, "partners in a flossy restaurant business with an ex-lover of my father's, Glen Thornton. My father cropped up again, promising Thornton love, but only taking money. Thornton is hung up on him. De Hooch found out what was going on and threatened to kill Eric if he didn't leave Thornton alone. Maybe de Hooch carried out his threat."

Sewell regarded me with pain.

"Then there's an actor, Sean Raftery, who had the best part in his life in that new film nailed down. Only my father slept with an agent named Toddy Niles, and Niles pried up the part and gave it to Eric. Raftery told everyone in the industry he wanted to kill Eric for that."

"You've been busy," Sewell said.

"Like you should have been," I said.

"I talked to the Payne woman. There's nothing there."

"All right. Did you talk to Niles? He had an affair going with a man in films, a casting director. And he broke it off when my father promised him lifelong affection if only he'd get him the part in the picture. Then, when he got it, he walked out on Niles. Couldn't Niles have resented that, maybe, just a little bit?"

Sewell scowled at me thoughtfully for a second. Then he set down his cup and stood up. "Come on," he said, and walked to the door. His jacket was hanging there. He took it down, put it on, and looked back at me. I got up and went after him. Downstairs, we got into a car that wasn't black and white like the others on the lot. It was plain beige.

"I want to show you something." Sewell steered up Wilcox, nudging the car along through clotted, home-going traffic. The side street he turned onto wasn't trafficky, but its few cars crawled anyway. So did ours. "I want you to look at the people along this street."

I looked. They were nearly all males, high school age, college age. Only most of them weren't school types—they were dropout types. There was quite a bit of long hair. There were bleached Levi's, workshirts with the arms ripped off, boots, bare feet. They walked slow, or lounged at corners. Always alone. A spaced-out string of them leaned against a chainlink fence edging a school playground where drooping pepper trees dropped dry leaves on the blacktop. Half a dozen sat apart from each other on the steps of a white colonial style church. Across from them, one perched on a fireplug. When a car passed, they looked at the car. The rest of the time, they looked at nothing.

"Hustlers," Sewell said. "Kids from nowhere, anywhere, here today, gone tomorrow. Any one of the men in any one of these cars can rent any one of them. For five, ten, twenty bucks, depending on variables—how goodlooking they are, how young, how new to town, how cooperative."

"They're peddling their ass?"

He nodded. "I've counted twenty-three of them in these four blocks." He turned the car around again. "And you come along, and name to me four people who might have killed your father." At a stoplight, he got out a cigarette, fitted it into a white mouthpiece, and pushed a dashboard lighter.

"And you wonder why I haven't done my job. If I'd done my job, if there was ever time to do any job, if some jobs were worth trying to do—"

The lighter clicked and he used it.

"—I wouldn't have stopped after I'd questioned half a dozen of these freaks. None of whom knew of any hustler who's split the scene suddenly following your father's death. I'd have questioned them all. Except that the one who did it, if one of them did, would have been in Albuquerque or Denver or Des Moines by then, shoving some other unlucky customer off a balcony, or beating his head in with a hammer."

He swung the car into the police parking lot.

"I wouldn't have taken you on this tour, but you already knew your father was homosexual. And I wanted you to understand where your ideas about murder could lead. Your father didn't have a regular sex partner—"

"I heard he did. But nobody could tell me his name."

"Exactly. The manager of the building where he lived told us he brought home hustlers." Sewell lifted a hand to fend me off. "I'm not putting him down. But that pattern is one a lot of homosexuals follow. And it's almost a sure way for them to end up beaten, robbed, and worse."

"Was he robbed?"

"No. Which brings us back to reality." He opened the door and stepped out.

I did the same. At the rear of the car, I squinted at Sewell against the harsh red glare of the sky. "But you admit he could have been murdered."

"There's no evidence."

"But you went to the funeral in case that hustler showed up."

Sewell sighed impatiently. "Alan, this isn't TV. In real life, people hurt themselves far more often than others hurt them. What happened to your father was probably as simple as something, some papers, say, blowing off the railing of that balcony. He made a grab for them, missed his footing, lost his balance, fell."

"Wonderful," I said. "Did you find any papers?"

"It didn't have to be papers," Sewell snapped.

"You keep making up excuses," I said.

He walked off.

Ocotillo Trail was a strip of patchy asphalt that bent its way up a little box canyon high in the hills off Cahuenga Pass. The ridges that bracketed the canyon were still bright, but down in the bottom, evening was grapejuice thick. Country mailboxes leaned shadowy against each other beside gates under clumps of big ragged trees. Back in the brush, windows glowed in scattered houses. A pair of kids rode horses home through the dusk. Creak of leather, solid clop of big hoofs. Someplace a dog barked. Sadder, and farther off, a rooster crowed.

I climbed around a corner, and up ahead, among huge old Japanese pines, houses climbed the canyon's box end, out of the shadows, into the light, the top windows mirroring the dying sun. They were really one loose structure, linked by walkways and stairs. They were beautiful—redwood frame with thick, square beams, deep eaves, porches. And like nothing you could see anywhere else. Strictly Southern California, pre World War I. I couldn't remember seeing this exact complex pictured in any architecture book, but it was that good.

I went up the first walkway, whose overhead beams dripped with cool blue wisteria blossoms. Wide, low-lift wooden steps got me to a long porch where ferns hung in wire baskets from beams, neglected, the fronds turning brown, drying out. Thumbtacked to a door was a crisp, new file card, lettered in felt pen—MANAGER TOP APARTMENT. I took a deep breath and started for steps at the far end of the porch, and noticed the windows I passed looked blank. I put my face to one, blinkering it with my hands. Vacant. Hardwood flooring gleamed dimly in the gloom. Far back, an inset of stained glass above a built-in sideboard glowed ruby, emerald, topaz.

I frowned, and turned to peer through the gathering dusk at the landscaping. Ghostly white roses nodded on canes that bowed to the earth. Foxtails sprouted bristly through the dense ground ivy. Honeysuckle climbed posts to the porch roof, where it piled and hung heavy off the eaves. Late as it was, bees still worked in it. One more load of pollen, then back to the hive. To sleep? I didn't think bees slept. I was leaning on the flat porch rail. My hands felt damp, and I saw dark rings on the rail where flower pots must have stood.

Puzzled by the vacancy and neglect, I began to climb. Tired and not happy. Maybe I was a little happier than before because Eric had chosen this place to live in, but generally I was disgusted with Eric and sick of him after all the talk from all the people I'd seen today. And yesterday. I wasn't sure anymore that it mattered what had happened to him, not sure why I felt like crying, thinking of him jumping, falling, being pushed screaming off here someplace, not sure it did make me feel like crying, not sure that maybe, by now, I wasn't like Lieutenant Sewell, simply uneasy at being ignorant, simply wanting answers. To what had happened. To why.

The wooden stairs were plain, solid, beautifully put together, and they never climbed too far before meeting a long landing or another long porch. On the second level, two of the three apartments were occupied. On the third, only one was. I passed it, and swung my legs over the porch rail in front of another of the vacant windows, vacant rooms. I breathed for a while, looking into the canyon, where the shadows were darkening like bruises, and the scattered lights looked farther apart and lonelier now. A mockingbird sang every tune he knew. When he quit, it was so still I could hear the dry needles sifting down through the big pines. Cool air came up out of the canyon bottom, smelling of sage.

I sighed, lifted my tired legs back over the rail, and trudged, heavy-footed, up the last flight of stairs, where runners from overhead bougainvillea brushed my face with dark red flowers. At the top, there was only one apartment. The last of the sunlight poured into it through a wide window that had no blinds. It showed me a tall young man in bluejeans, shirtless, barefoot, hair tied back like an Indian's, black straight hair. He was half turned away, mixing paint in a yellow plastic bucket on an upended packing case strewn with brushes, putty knives, tin cans, junk. At his feet, a paper bag leaked white plaster. Against the walls, that were paneled half-way up, and grass-papered above, leaned tall slabs of Masonite, hiding their faces. Another slab, smoothly plastered, was cleated to a big easel that was spotted with old paint. He began covering the plaster with red enamel. The door stood open. I tapped it with a knuckle, and he turned and looked at me. He stood very still, and paint dripped off the brush onto the floor like blood from a cut hand.

"The manager?" I said.

For a count of maybe ten, there was no answer. Then, "Yes, but you don't want to rent."

"I want to see Eric Tarr's apartment. I'm his son."

"Right." He leaned the brush in a coffee can, came nearer but not near, and studied me with eyes bright and hard to see into as black glass. There was a kind of hush to the way he moved. There was a hush to the way he stood there. When he spoke, it sounded easy but somehow careful. "This is it. I moved up here after—afterward. I get my choice now. Till the place is torn down."

"Torn down! Why? It's beautiful."

"Greene and Greene," he said. "1913. If this town had any pride or decency, they'd disassemble it, board by board, nail by nail, and move it someplace for people to look at. Forever. They won't. They'll just smash it. They're thirsty. They're putting in a reservoir here. Earth dam at the other end. There's been a lot of postponements while

114

the environmentalists scream, but it won't stop anything. They're going to do it."

"When did he move in? Did you know it then?"

"I told him." He went back to the packing case, the easel. I followed. "But he said he'd take the place anyway. He'd been here once in the sixties, at a party or something. Always dreamed of living here." He took the paintbrush out of the can and wiped thinner off it with a rag that was once a shirt. "The rents had been too high. Then he got a good part in a picture, and on a chance, he drove up here, and my foster father had already sold out to the Water District, and people had moved out, and this place was vacant, and he took it."

"What happened to his furniture?"

"The place was furnished. It's in storage. I don't need it." He began painting the Masonite again. He didn't work neatly. Paint splashed his chest, his flat belly, the bluejeans, his naked feet. He was the color of those brown eggs that cost extra at supermarkets, when they even have them. He was smooth all over. No extra weight on him, but he wasn't thin. Maybe he was some kind of Oriental—partly, anyway. "Go ahead," he said. "Look around if you want to."

Two steps led up to a dining area where cabinets were built in, Art Nouveau flowers and leaves leaded into glass doors that were exactly the right shape. There was a good kitchen. Something was warming in the oven. It smelled Mexican, and made me hungry. The staircase went up from the livingroom and took a single turn. The proportions were elegant, the wood was warm. There was a bathroom at the top, and to the left a big square bedroom with windows along two sides and French doors opening on a wooden balcony on the third side.

I hesitated, then I worked the latch and stepped out on the balcony and looked down. If Eric had gone off here, he'd fallen a lot farther than four floors. The slope dropped off steeply. In the twilight, outcrops of pale rock showed under the dark pines. They looked ready to break bones. I shivered, and turned around, and the tall boy was there in the doorway. I hadn't heard him come. He was watching me, and mopping paint off his chest with a rag that smelled of thinner.

"Was it here?" I asked.

He nodded. Nothing showed in his face.

"*Variety* printed that he fell out of a window. What kind of reporter would write that?"

"The kind that uses the phone and doesn't listen." He had his chin tucked in, looking down at his belly while he scrubbed the paint off. "No reporters came here. He was the only one that even called."

"The police came," I said. "You told them he brought home hustlers."

The wide, smooth shoulders rose and fell. "He was a fag." He turned and went back into the room. The bed was a wide mattress on a box spring on the floor, unmade, sheets and blankets tumbled. He sat on it, and bent to rub the paint off his feet. His voice came muted. "He sure as hell did bring home hustlers."

"What for?" I leaned in the doorway. "I was told he had a lover—a new, young lover."

116

His back straightened slowly. He raised his head. His mouth twisted in disbelief, and his voice scoffed. "Who? What was his name?"

"What's your name?"

"Sage. Sage Carruthers." He held up his hand for me to shake. It was big, but the grip was gentle. He gave a short laugh. "They didn't say I was his lover, did they?"

"Were you?" I asked.

He stood up, grinning, and faced me, holding out his hands at his sides. "Do I look like a fag?"

"I don't know what a fag looks like. No. They didn't tell me his name. Nobody had met him. Eric had just told them about him."

"Told who? That Payne woman? The one with the deep-freeze face? He'd tell her anything." Sage crossed the landing to the bathroom. He pissed noisily. Over the noise he called, "And she'd believe anything he told her. Really pitiful."

A wide mirror covered the wall at the head of the bed. I stared into it. "Did she come here much?"

"Only afterward. Then she made a pest of herself, trying to claim stuff, stuff that wasn't even his, pots, pans, anything." The toilet flushed, and he came back, zipping his fly. He grinned at me in the mirror. "That was his. He must have liked to watch while he made out. He had a good body for past forty." Sage breathed a wry laugh. "She didn't ask for the mirror."

"I don't think she likes mirrors," I said.

Sage sniffed his armpits. "I need a shower." Under the windows, orange crates were stacked against the walls with books and records. There was a cheap, unpainted pine chest. Out of this he took a black T-shirt and black jeans. "Lover!" He shut the drawer. "What did he need with a lover? He could buy sex when he needed it." He dropped his pants and stepped out of them. Naked, he was as beautiful as Tombstone. "That was how he was—someone who bought things, not someone who loved things." He started out, then turned. "That's no special put down of your old man. This whole city is like that. The whole rotten country." He went out and into the bathroom. "Stay for supper," he called.

We sat on apple boxes and ate off a dropleaf table, using Navy surplus forks and plates that could have come from Joanna Payne's shop, except they'd never been that dirty. The food was tamale pie. Sage had baked it himself, using a recipe off a cornmeal box, and it was good. He shoveled it in, washing it down with glasses of red wine from a gallon jug. I didn't do so well. Something had gone wrong with my swallowing mechanism.

Because, while Sage showered, I had left the bedroom. It bothered me—the French doors standing open to that balcony, the mirror giving me back the empty reflection of the unmade bed. I went downstairs. The big room was shadowy by then. The Masonite on the easel was glossy with red enamel. I stood and stared at it, and at the packing case worktable, because they were all there was to look at. Then I saw the open back of the packing case, and rolls of paper leaning in it, and sheets of paper of different sizes lying in it. With drawings on them. I sat on the floor to look at the drawings.

The top ones I couldn't make out, irregular shaded patches on tracing paper. But when I got down into the stack, I saw they were the shadow elements of a picture of a human face—the shapeless rounds of eye sockets, the triangle next to the nose, the rectangular inlet under the mouth. Each drawing of the series grew more detailed. The last was a careful pencil mock of a photograph. Out of the eyes, my father looked at me. The noise of the water climbing the old plumbing to the bathroom stopped. I put the drawings back . . .

Now Sage looked at me across the table. "This is the only food there is," he said. "Unless you want crackers and peanutbutter."

"No." I tangled my fork in the sticky Jack cheese that topped the chili-red mess on my plate, and made myself look happy chewing it and gulping it down. "This is great."

"Try the wine. It's very good cheap vino. You can't find this brand everyplace."

"I'm not used to drinking," I said. "Can I ask you something?"

He nodded about a sixteenth of an inch.

I said, "Apartment managers are fat and sixty-five, and they always have a three day stubble of beard, and they sit in front of a television set drinking beer around the clock, and the only time they get up is to go to the bathroom, and they resent even that."

"I'm still the manager," Sage said, and went to the stove for more food. "See, there was this art school here in L.A. I thought I wanted to go to. I got my foster father to send me. I was adopted when I was six. He had a wife then, but he didn't keep her. He kept me because there wasn't any way not to. Every once in a while, when I reminded him, he noticed me." He came back with his plate filled again, and straddled his apple box, and picked up the jug and sloshed the wine around in it. "Drink up, man."

I took a couple of swallows, and Sage splashed my glass full again. The amount of wine still left in that jug made me feel depressed.

"He didn't like being reminded much, so he did the second kind act of his life and let me come here. But in order for me to, like, pay my way, I had to look after the place for him." He showed me the edge of a smile. "Hell, he probably already knew he was going to sell. He wouldn't have trusted me with any real responsibility. Anyhow"—he shrugged—"it was free rent, and with allowance he was letting me have, I needed everything I could get free. Then I saw this place, and I could have hugged the old bastard. Except, he didn't know what he was doing. To him it was just a collection of old rundown shacks he'd picked up cheap. Hell, he never even heard of Greene and Greene. To him, an architect is just a highpriced blueprint maker."

"It's a big place," I said. "Wasn't it heavy, running it and going to school too?"

"School? Shit, they couldn't have been unhappier about me if I'd painted with my cock. I was there exactly three days."

"And your foster father doesn't care?"

"He's in New Mexico in a wheelchair. He never

comes here. He doesn't know what the hell I'm doing. Neither do I. Except I'm painting. Which I'd be doing if I was in art school—only not my way. It can't hurt him—he's got the bread. Cotton and oil. It's no good to him. He's half dead. Always was." Sage chuckled, and in the dusk of the kitchen, I saw the gleam of his teeth. "Come to think of it, I do paint with my cock." He gulped wine. "So did Picasso."

"Pictures of my father?"

Sage had lowered his glass to within an inch of the table top. He held it there. He blinked at me. He set the glass down. He rubbed his mouth with the back of his hand. "Why not?" He shrugged. "He was gone on himself. Actors always are. He asked me to paint him. That's what the red board is for." He dug into the food on his plate again. He talked with his mouth full. "You saw the drawings—right?" He swallowed. "Well, they go across in rows." He held his hands apart to show the size of the drawings. He moved them, like framing squares of air. "The image gets a little clearer with each one, red on red, with almost no contrast to start with"—he took another mouthful—"then darkening the contrast till the one with the most detail is nearly black. Then the snapshot one"—he swallowed again—"in the bottom right hand corner. Comprendo?"

"Except he'll never see it," I said.

"I'll see it," Sage said.

"Why? He was nothing to you. Was he?"

Sage reached for my plate, set it on his own, collected the forks and got up. He scraped what I had left on my plate back into the pan on the stove.

"He was nothing to me." He turned on hot water at the sink and cleaned the serving spoon and the forks with his fingers, and mopped the plates with his hand, and set them steaming in a rack of rubber coated wire on the drainboard. "The picture is something to me." He turned off the faucet. "It's going to be a good picture." He wiped his hands on a ragged gingham towel and set the ruins of the tamale pie in an old refrigerator that was nearly empty and whose lightbulb had gone out. "Stick around for a few days. You'll see." He hooked a finger through the handle of the wine jug. He picked up his apple box. "Come on," he said.

I followed him upstairs. At the top, he set the apple box down and handed me the jug. I held it while he climbed up on the box and pushed open a trap in the ceiling. When his hand came out of the dark, it held a battered coffee can. Without closing the hatch, he jumped down. The can rattled when he dropped it on the bed. There was more daylight in the bedroom than downstairs but it was still dusky and fading fast, and I couldn't see for sure, but what seemed to be in the can were bent, rusty nails. Sage brought out of a closet a black, fake leather case, set it on the chest of drawers, and opened it. It was a stereo player with two speakers in the split lid. He set the speakers apart, crouched to plug in the power cord, then sat on the bed and shuffled record albums from the orange crates. "What do you want to hear?"

"Bach," I said.

"Rock," he said, "right. Whose?"

"Johann Sebastian Bach," I said.

But it was the Grateful Dead, whispering and hooting and whining in a reverberation of guitars, like little kids scaring each other with echoes in a dark culvert. Sage sat on the bed again, dug out of the nails in the coffee can a leather pouch like Gus's, found a little blue folder of papers, and rolled a cigarette. Fast and neat, like a 1930's Republic Pictures bad man. He even closed the thong drawstring of the pouch with his teeth. Kitchen matches lay scattered on an orange-crate shelf. He lit one with a thumbnail, and blew out the flame with smoke from the cigarette. Then he held the cigarette out to me. I dragged on it. The smoke was the same kind, but not so rough as had come from Gus's. Maybe the ingredients were better. I held the smoke.

Sage stretched out on the bed, hands folded behind his head on the pillows, legs crossed at the ankles. "Why did you go to the cops?"

I let the smoke out. "I don't think he fell, I don't think he jumped, I think somebody pushed him."

"And the nice policeman is there to help us?"

"I went to everybody else first." I passed back the cigarette, leaned against the book-filled orange crates, and told Sage about Thornton, de Hooch, Toddy Niles, Joanna Payne, and Raftery. I described the men carefully. "Did any of them ever come here?"

"Just hustlers from Selma street," he said. "You don't have to stand up. Lie down."

My mouth felt dry. I squatted for the wine jug and unscrewed the cap. "You know a lot about him."

"My place was down below. There's only one way

in. I saw everybody that came. Hey, man, come on, lie down."

I tilted up the jug and drank awkwardly, set the jug down and put its cap back on. "It's the wrong bed," I said.

Sage passed me the cigarette. "You're strung out about him, aren't you?"

I walked to the French doors and stared out into the shaggy darkness of the pines. "I don't know why," I said. "My mother says he was a shit." I worked at sounding sorry for myself. "He never cared about me. In my whole life he never wrote a letter or made a phone call or came to see me. He was a shadow on a picture tube, that was all. My father. And then he broke his neck down there, and I felt sorry. I really felt lost, all of a sudden, really alone."

"I know what you mean." Sage was standing right behind me. "I never even had a father. Some horny kid soldier living it up in Saigon one night." He touched my hand to get the cigarette back. He sucked the smoke out of the last inch of it. He was so close I could feel the heat of him. "Well, look," he said softly, "don't believe your mother. Or what I told you, either. He wasn't a shit. He was beautiful. I mean," he added quickly, defensively, "sure, he was gay. So naturally I never knew him well, did I? We weren't close, okay? But—"

I turned and put my mouth on Sage's mouth.

For a second, Sage stood rigid with surprise. Then the little red coal of the cigarette dropped and lay bright on the bare floor, and his arms came around me and closed me hard against him. His mouth, sweet from the smoke and sour from the wine, was hungrier on my mouth than it had been downstairs, stowing away the tamale pie. It grew hard for me to breathe. I made a sound, and Sage broke the kiss. His eyes shone. Tears had made tracks down his face.

"Jesus," he whispered. "Ah, Jesus."

"Surprise," I said.

He laughed shakily. With a tenderness you'd use to touch a child, his hands pushed back my hair and held my head on either side. "Yeah, surprise. Like, I was about to die here. Then there you were. Only you didn't help. Looking just like him"—he touched my lips with his—"then coming down that way on queers. You make me cry. I can't help crying." He sniffed and wiped his nose on his arm. "Come on." He tugged up my T-shirt. I raised my arms and he worked the shirt carefully off over my head, and tossed it into the shadows. Then I did it for him. His skin felt as smooth as it looked, and he was very warm.

Like Gus's, his fingers wedged open the steel button of my Levi's and slid the zipper. He knelt and dragged down my pants. He pried off my shoes, then stood again, with a little asking smile, so I unlatched his pants and pushed them down. Sage was barefoot, so all he had to do was step out of them. Then he held me again. He was very strong. I didn't want it to feel good but it felt good. Maybe the way it would feel to have your father hold you. Only you wouldn't be naked, of course, his cock wouldn't be hard, and he wouldn't be rummaging around in the dark of your mouth with his tongue.

He took my hands and, walking backward, led

me to the bed. He sat down, lay back dark across the dim whiteness of the sheets, held out his arms for me. And I saw the pale ghost of my little bare-ass self in the mirror, and that made it real, and I couldn't move anymore. I could only stare and feel coldness spread out through me from someplace deep in my belly. Sage got off the bed, yanked one of the sheets free, stood on the bed and hung the sheet across the mirror.

He jumped down off the bed, took hold of my shoulders very tenderly, and kissed me very tenderly on the mouth, and let his hands slide down to take my hand, and very tenderly draw me down onto the bed, to lie against him and get heat from him, like the old king in the Bible. David? They brought him a young girl. I tried to picture Sage, holding me as if I were a shivering little kid, mouth to mouth, big hands smoothing my back—tried to picture him as a young girl. Like Gus. Bad news— I couldn't. Worse news—I didn't need to. My reflexes didn't know the difference. My physiology acted the same as if Sage had been a girl. And my so-called mind, the brilliant best part of me? All it could do was think that this was what it was like to be my father, in my father's bed. Alive—no coffin, no cold, wet flowers, no lonely grave.

But I didn't know the moves. Sage did. Sage made the moves. For a long while. Then it came my turn. Sage rolled away from me and lay there, sprawled on his back in the dark, panting, gasp-ing, laughing softly to himself, pleased. He was glossed with sweat. The smell of his sweat was like a new knife, clean, edgy. His hand reached and found my hand and put it on him. And it was my turn. I took a deep breath, lowered my head, and tried. But even when you know you have to, you don't do well what you're scared of doing. And I made mistakes and fumbled, and Sage stopped me. He lifted my head and frowned down into my eyes.

"You never did any of this before," he said.

I swallowed. "I'm sorry if it's no good."

"It's good, but you're not doing it because you want to. What are you doing it for?"

"For you," I lied, "because you want me to. Because he's dead, and he can't do it, and I look like him, and you loved him." I moved to go on with what I'd been doing, but Sage wouldn't let me.

"No." He rolled fast off the bed. "No." He stood silhouetted against the pale darkness of the open French doors, looking down. "I can't let you. You don't want to. Not for me. Because—yes, right, I loved him. But I killed him. I killed him."

The Grateful Dead left off jibbering in their echo chamber. The record player clicked, turning itself off. The sheet covering the mirror slithered down. I saw myself, small and naked and stiff with shock, on my hands and knees in the middle of the bed. Dim. And very scared. Because it was too soon. I wasn't ready. Christ, we were alone up here. And Sage was big, and in a second he was going to realise what he'd said. And that balcony was right behind him, and the long drop into the dark, and the breakneck rocks waiting.

"Come on, man," I said shakily.

"It's true," Sage said. "You knew it right away."

"Ah, listen—" I made myself get off the bed and

reach out to him. He backed off. "Make sense," I said. "Why? Why would you kill him?"

"Because he loved me." Sage swung away and put his hands out, high, to grip the doorframe, and leaned there, his back to me, his head hanging, like a kind of crucifixion. "And I treated him—" his voice broke. "Shit, I didn't mean it. Didn't mean anything. I was stupid, that's all." He covered his face with his hands and sobbed. "Dumb, kid stupid."

I was afraid to move, but I moved. I put my hands on his jerking ribs and turned him, and pulled him close so he was crying on my shoulder. I stroked his back. "Easy," I said. "Easy, Sage." He shuddered and hung on tight. "Come on, man," I told him. "Don't cry."

He sniffled and wiped his nose on his arm again, and let himself be led back to sit on the side of the bed. He really looked sad, hunched forward, head drooping, hands hanging between his naked knees. He really sounded sad, hiccuping, trying to stop crying. I sat next to him and stroked his back. I didn't want to. I wanted to grab my pants off the floor and run like hell down all those stairs, stairs, stairs. But I couldn't.

I asked, "What was it you didn't mean?"

He shrugged and gave a jerky sigh. His voice was wobbly. "When he came here"—he gulped—"I didn't know anything about it." He touched my thigh. "You know? What we've been doing?" He lay across the bed to grope for tissues in one of the orange crates. He blew his nose, and sat up, cross-legged, in the middle of the bed. "It never passed through my mind that I could be, like, gay, all right? And then, there he was, and he, well, he just kind of made it happen. I mean, ah, Christ, what a beautiful, easy dude. Afterward, I didn't feel any different, didn't feel, well"—he shrugged, trying to find words—"like a faggot. I mean, we did it a lot. And it was just—good, you know? I mean, having somebody hold you?" He looked at me.

I nodded and faked an answer. "Like tonight."

"Was it?" His eyes picked up shine from somewhere. He smiled a little, and reached for my hand. I gave it to him. He said, "Yeah, like that. I never had anybody love me. Whores in Albuquerque, that's all. You know, in high school you have to try the whores. Peer group pressure—right? Beat up queers in gay bar parking lots, too. Same reason. But the whores—that's not love. I didn't know anything about love. I wasn't mature about it. I mean, sex was still something separate and apart, okay? And what we were doing—Eric and me—well, I mean, that was far out, you know? Kinky, wasn't it? Not real L-O-V-E." He gave a bitter laugh at himself. "I mean, he was a man, understand? And I was a man. Men don't *love* other *men*, for Christ sake. You see where my head was?"

I saw, all right. I nodded.

"The trouble was, I got hooked on it. I'd never have admitted it, but I really dug it. I mean, we were at it, seemed like, all the time. I was up here every night. Afternoons sometimes, mornings too. But I kept telling myself it didn't mean anything. I was alone here, didn't know anybody, didn't know where to meet anybody—didn't have time, too busy painting. And he wanted it. So—big deal. It beat jacking off.

"I thought I was cool, see? I wasn't. I was hot as

a two dollar pistol. For him. And when it got to me—the truth, I mean—that I was in love with him, really strung out, couldn't think of anything else, I got shook, really shook. I couldn't face it. No, I said, it's only sex. I can do that with anybody. I'm nobody's possession, you know? And I didn't need anybody—no one person. That dependency shit, that's deadly, you know?"

I stared. "That's why you killed him?"

"What?" He jerked with shock. The bed jerked. "Oh, no, man, you don't understand. Let me tell you. There was this woman at the art school. I mean, you know, everybody was kids there. Your age, my age, but she was old. I don't mean old—she was like forty, maybe. In good shape, though. And, if you didn't look too close, beautiful. Not that she used a lot of makeup—she didn't. She kept her face clean and didn't do anything fancy with her hair. Neat but not gaudy, like they say.

"She wore sort of handwoven stuff, wrap around skirts, leather sandals, always big beads and pendants, you know, hoop earrings, woven belts? She did pottery, but she was at the school to get her drawing straight. It was a life class. I had it too. She had the bench next to me and we talked a lot. She kept after me. Anywhere around the school she found me, she always talked to me. And when she talked to you, she touched you, right? And I wasn't too bright, but pretty soon I figured out what it was all about, but I didn't let on I understood. She wasn't—"

He let the sentence drop. He took a deep breath.

"But when I got scared of how I was hung up on Eric and what we were doing, I thought of her. And I went back to the school. There's an eating place across the street where everybody goes for hamburgers and Cokes and coffee, and I went at noon and hung around, and she didn't show up. But the next day she did. And I told her about what I was painting, and she said she'd like very much to see it, she thought I had genius, and was sorry when I left the school, but I was probably right, they couldn't teach anybody with talent like mine anything, and a lot of beautiful bullshit like that. So I brought her up here and wow! I mean, she was wild. I hardly had a chance to make a pass, and we were naked on the floor. Never even got near the bedroom. And we're banging away like fifty carpenters, when I look up, and there's Eric, standing in my doorway."

"You didn't kill him," I said.

"It's the same as if I did. He turned white around the mouth. I mean, white, man. Did you ever see that happen? It's scary. It made me feel sick. Because I wasn't doing this with this woman to show him anything. He was supposed to be at some recording studio doing overdubbing for his picture. I wasn't even going to tell him. I was just doing it to show myself is all—that I was all right, you know, didn't need him, wasn't queer.

"And him standing there, crying, saying he loved me, and he thought I loved him, and how could I do this to him—it blew my mind. I went crazy. I told him I didn't love anybody. Nobody owned me. I'd do it with whoever I wanted, whenever I wanted. And it wouldn't be with any more studs, either. Because I wasn't queer, did he understand that? I was really screaming at him by then. *I'm not queer!*"

"He killed himself," I said.

"It's the same thing," Sage said stubbornly, hopelessly, tears in his voice. "It's the same fucking thing. I should have gone after him, should have told him it was lies, cover-up, fakery. I could have explained Eloise. He would have believed me. He would have understood. And it would have been all okay again. It would have been better than ever. But I couldn't. After Eloise took off, crying and red in the face and sore as hell and scared and frustrated and half a dozen other things—and I was alone there and, like, out of my skull. I must have walked to my door twenty times—to go up to him, to say I was sorry, to admit what I was and how I felt about him. I couldn't. All that old garbage they teach you was too heavy. I got juiced on wine and cried a lot, but I didn't go. I passed out. Next morning, I went. Sure, I did. But it was too late. He wasn't up here. He was dead down there under the trees. He'd been lying out there all night—dead."

"I better go." I got off the bed.

"No, please." Sage knelt up, reaching out, begging. "Don't go. I didn't mean for it to happen. I loved him. Please try to understand. I didn't mean it."

I picked up my pants. I felt hollow. "I understand."

"Don't hate me." He scrambled off the bed and started to reach for me and stopped himself. Tears spilled silver down his face. "Don't hate me."

"I don't hate you," I said. "You're the only one that ever knew him that I like. That's freaky, no? If any of them had killed him, I'd have killed them. You killed him—you couldn't help it, but you did.

Maybe I'd have acted the same way. Anyway, I don't hate you. I can't. I just feel"—in a second, I was going to start crying too—"sorry. So damn sorry."

"Love me?" he said, and touched me, touched my chest, a very light touch. His voice was thin, a little kid's. "I don't want to be alone anymore. I want—when you walked in that door, it was like he was back. All new. And I could do it right this time. Stay with me. I want. I need." He took the pants out of my hand and let them fall. He stepped close, so that our mouths touched. His mouth felt cold and forlorn and tasted of the salt from his tears. "Please? Love me?"

What could I tell him? That I wasn't queer? Not after what he'd told me. It would sound like a tinny echo. It didn't help that it was true. He wouldn't believe it. Why would he? I'd already done it with him, hadn't I—at least half. I'd started it. All I could tell him was the truth, that it had been a dirty trick, that all I'd done it for was to trap him. I couldn't say it. Not just because it made me ashamed. I was scared of what he'd do to me. I brushed his mouth with mine.

"Let's do it," I said.

When I dropped off the Greyhound bus onto the dirt shoulder of the highway at sunset, the fake California Mission archway to the trailer park looked about the same as when I'd left. Maybe another chunk of stucco had been knocked loose by a bad driver, but that happened a lot. I hadn't been gone long—it only seemed that way. My suitcase was in my hand again. It felt light. I wished I did. I didn't. I stood and stared at the beer billboard on the other side of the highway, with its props deep in dry brush, and felt as if my belly were full of cold rocks.

I had meant to leave Sage, Greene and Greene, Los Angeles, and everybody in it, in the morning. But I hadn't left. All that day, Sage and I lay naked on that rumpled bed in the heat, with wine and those hand-rolled cigarettes of his, and his sadness and my remorse, and Sage being unable to keep off me, and I being unable really to hate having him on me. At sunset, I'd said:

"I have to go."

"You have to eat," Sage said, and took me in his grimy fifties convertible with its knocked back roof in strips that flapped in the wind, took me not toward Hollywood where I could catch a bus, but to a plate-glass place in Cahuenga Pass for cheap steaks and French fries and ketchup, and then, when we were in the car again, back to the canyon.

"I want to go to the bus station," I said.

But Sage got tears in his eyes and begged me to stay. I could just have walked off. But I didn't. Following him up the stairs, I blamed the wine and the marijuana. They were messing up my head. I was having identity problems again. I was being my father for Sage's sake, and I was also being Sage, wasn't I, the way Sage had been when Eric found him? Which was dangerous, and I knew it was dangerous. But I let Sage take my clothes off me in the bathroom while the shower ran and, hating the begging look in his eyes, let myself take the clothes off Sage.

134

He washed me in the shower, in the steam, soaping me all over, slow, and getting a charge for himself. The feel of his hands smearing the slippery lather around on me gave me a charge too. I'd never felt anything so sexy. But then, what did I know? We stood facing each other with the water slopping our hair in our eyes, and Sage poked the soap into my hands, and I did for him what he had done for me, and when I got to where he was stiff, I laughed and pumped him with my slick fist, and he laughed too.

But something different was in his black eyes, something serious. He took my hand off him, kissed me, solemn and hungry, took back the soap and turned me around. He soaped my butt, deep, then pulled me back against him. No. Not Piper again. Never. I twisted away sharply, slipped on the soapy tiles, my feet went out, and I was sitting flat, looking up at Sage.

"What's wrong?" he said. "It won't hurt. I promise. Don't be scared. You'll like it. It feels good."

"I won't like it, Sage," I said, and reached up and cranked off the shower, and told him about Piper, the whole story. Without saying anything, he got out of the shower and dried himself. I pushed to my feet, got out after him. He handed me the towel, very glum. It made me feel guilty. And all that second night, I did nothing to stop Sage doing whatever he wanted—except that, of course—and, blaming the wine and the grass, I did nothing to stop myself from copying the things Sage did.

But when he woke me next morning, sitting naked on the side of the bed, holding mugs of coffee, I told him again, "I'm going."

"You can't. I love you. I need you. You love me too. You know it. Don't go. Don't do it to me."

"What about me?" I said. "What I'm doing to myself. You won't believe this, but I'm not gay. Honest."

He smiled the way I had known he would, the sad, cynical smile that said I was the same scared kind of liar to myself Sage had been to himself when he'd lied the lie that killed Eric. "Drink your coffee," he said. "I like the way your mouth tastes after coffee."

I sat up in the middle of the tangled sheets and took and drank from the mug but, "I'm really going," I said.

And Sage smiled and shook his head. He took the mug away from me, set it on the crates, pushed me back gently so I lay flat and began nuzzling my belly, and then took my cock in his mouth. And by reflex I touched his hair, that long, smoky, girl hair of his, stroked it, combed it with my fingers while his head bobbed, and he hummed. Habit. Already. So soon. I pushed him off.

"Look," I said loudly, "I do have to go. I have to."

"Why?" He sat up, frowning. "You don't hate it. So you're straight. Maybe I'm straight too. Maybe everybody's straight. Maybe nobody. There's so much stupidity mixed up with sex, Alan. Political stupidity, historical stupidity, religious stupidity. You have to get it out of your mind. You can't live with it. It'll wreck your life. It's wrecking the whole world."

"My mother expected me back days ago."

"Your mother!" Sage laughed.

136

I wanted my clothes. "You don't know it—but Eric left her for this, what we've been doing." I got off the bed. "I can't do it to her too. Twice in a lifetime?"

"Do what to her?" He reached up and caught my arm. "You plan to spend the rest of your life with your mother?"

"I don't know about the rest of my life." I jerked away from him. "All I know is now. And now I can't do it to her." I found my pants crumpled and damp on the bathroom floor. I kicked into them fast. "Take me to the bus station."

"Walk!" he yelled. "Walk to the goddam bus station." And he started to cry again.

"Don't do that," I said. "It's not fair. Do you want me for a fucking prisoner, is that what you want?" I took out my comb and worked at my hair in the mirror, and Sage bent and picked up my T-shirt off the floor and held it for me to put on. Mute. The silence was sadder than the crying. I pushed the comb away. I poked my arms into the shirt and ducked my head, and Sage put it on for me and smoothed it down. I tucked it into my pants and then we stood facing each other with our hands hanging and stared into each other's eyes. I told myself that if he tried to kiss me, I'd bite his mouth. He didn't try. He turned away. It made my chest hurt. The words came out before I could stop them.

"Kiss me?" I said. "Kiss me, Sage?"

Sage looked at me, shook his head, and started down the stairs. "No. You want me to kiss you goodbye. I won't kiss you goodbye. . . ."

Now I trudged between the rows of mobile

homes, the clash of television racket, the mix of supper smells, the whines and cries of children and the yap of dogs, to find Babe. But another trailer was parked where ours used to be—one in much better shape. I squinted at it for a stupid length of time. A fat little girl about four years old, in a tight gingham sunsuit, came out the door singing to herself and patting her hair absent-mindedly with a pink popsickle. She looked at me as if she were Miss Muffet and I were the spider, and ran back inside the trailer, making scared noises. I went away.

The Casa Camino was cold. You couldn't depend on the food but you could depend on the air conditioning. Half an acre of candle-lit tables stretched away white and empty under the carved, painted rafters. Reflected in fake antique gold crackle-back mirrors, the Mexican waiters stood around murmuring in green jackets. It was too early to eat and too late to drink. Almost. A few customers still sat on high leather-cushioned stools at the tooled leather bar and moved their mouths in jokes they wouldn't remember tomorrow. Recorded music no one would remember tomorrow whispered in the chill. No one sat at the Baldwin in the diningroom. The bartender looked like a doll you wind up and it grows old.

"Where's Babe?" I asked him.

"Alan!" The bartender smiled mechanically. "Did you lose your calendar, *querido*? Babe don't work on Monday."

"She's moved," I said. "Do you know where?"

In a pile of business cards and IOU's on scraps of paper next to the candle-lit cash register, he found a scrap that he showed me. An address was written on it. It had to be Babe's. The ink was purple.

The street was new, like the stucco boxes that lined it. Grass and dichondra were just taking hold, like green mange, on the square, fertilizer-perfumed front yards. The trees were young, skinny, and propped too straight with steel pipe splints tied by no-color rags. Smoke drifted past, with the smell of charred beef. And from somewhere, gunfire sounded. I stopped. But no one came out of front doors looking alarmed. I went on. The gunfire rattled again. It came from back of the house I wanted. I knew I wanted it because Babe's trailer stood in the driveway. No one was inside. I pressed a disk of plastic pearl next to the front door of the house. No one came. I walked up the driveway.

Babe was there in the back yard, all right. She was beautiful. In low-waisted blue slacks and one of those bare midriff things, half shirt, half bra. White, printed with little red and blue stars. She was grilling hamburgers at a raw brick barbecue, and serving them on paper plates to women who looked like they let their smiles out only once a week. Their men were crew-cut and beefy, athletes from high schools long torn down. They stood in a row, and shot pellet pistols at a target moving on a chainbelt against a cinder-block wall at the end of the yard. It was noisy. No one seemed to mind. The target was a very old painted sheet metal cutout of a caricature Negro bent over and running scared with a chicken under his arm. It traveled jerkily and fast, and they potted at it, and laughed, and tilted beer down their thick throats till the target came around again. The women laughed too. Babe laughed. I went over to her. She cocked an eyebrow at me while she spooned pickle relish onto buns.

"Well," she said. "Where have you been?"

"There were complications," I said.

The women had knobs at the hinges of their jaws that moved when they chewed. The knobs stopped moving while they stared at me. Babe introduced me and they shook hands like men, they smiled like men. The men didn't smile. They looked down at me as if I were one of those fish that has to be thrown back because it's too small. They herded like feedlot steers around the barbecue chimney for hamburgers, potato chips, cole slaw. I took a plate too, even though I'd lost my appetite.

It was another half hour before I could get Babe alone. In a Montgomery Ward livingroom, where the lampshades still had on their clear plastic wrappers.

"What's happening?" I asked her.

"Do you know," she said, "that when you went to Eric's funeral was the first time you've ever spent a night out of that trailer?" It wasn't accurate, but I didn't interrupt. "Well, it was. And do you know, you are no longer a little boy? And you'll soon be grown up and gone, right out of my life? You'll have your own wife and kids and your own troubles. And do you know what I'll be then? An old lady nobody gives a damn for."

"You've been thinking," I said.

Her smile was crooked and wise. "You didn't

know I could, did you, baby? Well, I can. And it came over me that nobody's going to look out for Babe Tarr but Babe Tarr herself. Luther's been pestering me to marry him since last summer. I thought, what the hell. He's a cop. Nothing's steadier than that. He'll be chief someday, too. I'll tell him yes."

"I've only been gone a couple of days," I said. "If I'd stayed a month, who would you have married—Colonel Qaddafi?"

She narrowed her eyes. "I don't know who that might be, but I expected you to understand my position. People aren't going to want an old witch playing the piano in their bars. I don't know what you're going to do for a living. With all those brains, teach college, I suppose. But one thing I do know. You're not going to want to be saddled with me. Anyway, I'm not getting any younger, and I'm entitled to some happiness."

"You're entitled to all you can get," I said. "I love you, Babe. Did you know that?"

She patted me cheek and kissed me lightly. "I know. That's sweet. But it's not quite what I meant."

"Right," I said. "Where did you get that target?"

"Bought it from a broken down amusement pier down the coast somewhere. Isn't it cute?"

"Darling," I said. "Are you married already?"

"Next Sunday," she said. "You can give me away." She got up. "Come on. I'll show you your room. It's very cozy. And I bought you a bookcase. Luther couldn't get over it."

I couldn't get over it either. It had two shelves. They were calling Babe from the yard, and she went back out there, and I sat down on the cozy bunk bed and cried for a while. I ended up not staying. I wasn't giving her away. Not to Luther Schlag. Besides, I didn't have a suit to wear to a wedding.

The neon-circled clock in the shut-up service station where I'd gone the other day, after Piper raped me, told me it was three-forty-five. I left the lighted corner and followed the dark side street that led over the hump-back bridges. There was the vacant lot where the old car still crouched on its rusty axles in the weeds. Air was coming off the sea, smelling of dead plankton, but it didn't move enough to stir the greasy water of the canal that lay flat and black under a flat, black sky.

I followed the ragged cement edge of the canal till I found the house of Gus and Piper and Hughie and the rest. No light showed—not from it, any more than from the other cupcake-color houses that were no-color in the night. I stood and stared at it for a while. No van was parked beside it. I walked around the house, pushing thick lantana out of the way. At the back, I found the window of Gus's room, the one Piper had come crawling in through from guitar practice the other day. The window was too high off the ground for me to see through.

I stumbled around in the dark back yard and found a flabby tire mounted on a wheel, and leaned this under the window and stepped up on it. The window was closed, but the yellow cotton curtains were pulled back, and I could see the mattress in the corner, the scene of my deflowering, pale, a memory. Was anybody on it? I couldn't tell. But I was afraid Piper might be. I got down off the tire and walked around to the front of the house and stepped up on the stoop to peer through the door. I put my hands against the glass to shut out reflections, and the door gave a creak and fell in. Flat. With a very loud noise.

I ran. I crouched down, dry-mouthed, in the lantana, waiting. I didn't know what for, but whatever it was, it didn't happen. No one had heard me. I went back and reached in and found a light-switch. The table top had been pushed off its props, the can with the glass flowers and pussywillows was smashed, the fat colored candle kicked to pieces. The rock album posters had been ripped down and torn in strips. The sitar was splinters in the fireplace. The wooden beads of the former curtain were all over the floor. And in the room where the sleeping little kid with the cold had been, there was nothing but electronic junk. Shards of bright plastic and tangles of strings and knobs were all that was left of the guitars. The drums had been stamped through. The fronts of speaker-amplifiers had been kicked in. Transistors and diodes crunched under my shoes like gravel.

I wanted to feel pleased. I couldn't.

Sage lay on his back with the sheet under one leg and over the other, lay with his arms out and his mouth parted, snoring a little, troubled, maybe, because sometimes he rolled his head and whimpered. For a long time, while day made pale grey promises outside the open windows, open French doors, I stood and watched him. Then I went and sat on the side of the bed and undressed and lay beside him and kissed the long hair that sleep had strung across his face. He didn't open his eyes. His mouth tried to find mine.

"Eric?"

"Alan." I kissed him. "Say, 'Welcome, Alan.' "

A corner of his mouth smiled. "Welcome, Alan."

"Say, 'I want you, Alan.' "

"Mmm." He nodded and raked the hair off his face, and found my mouth again. "I want you, Alan."

"Say, 'I need you, Alan.' "

He rubbed his beard-stubbly face in my belly. "I need you, Alan." He looked up, and his black eyes were shiny. "I love you, Alan."

"No," I said, "that's not next. Next you say, 'I want you to live with me and never go away.' "

Sage made a face, tired of the routine.

"Say it!" I shouted, and started to cry, started and couldn't stop. "Say it, God damn it!"

"Hey." Sage took me in his arms and held me and stroked me till I stopped. "Okay." He whispered a laugh. "Let's see—'I want you to live with me and never go away.' Was that it? Did I get it right? Because I don't want anybody else saying it."

"Right." I wiped my nose on the sheet. Sage found Kleenex and blotted my tears with it. I took it and blew my nose. Sage gave me a worried grin.

"That all, now?"

I nodded. "Now you can say the other."

"I love you," Sage said.

" 'Alan'," I said. " 'I love you, Alan'."

Sage looked solemn. "I love you, Alan."

"I love you too," I said.

Sage clowned looking stern. "Aren't you forgetting? You're straight."

"Like you," I said, and laid my head in Sage's lap. Sage touched my hair.

"You were gone a long time."

I mumbled, "Twenty-two hours."

"We'll never get them back," Sage said.

"I have to get them back," I said. "I didn't sleep. Let me sleep? Right here?"

Sage let me.

The apartments emptied. The canyon emptied. There were no more sounds of cars and televisions, horses, kids, dogs, roosters—only crickets at night and birds during the day, and the wind in the pines. And the sounds of Sage and me—talk and laughter ricocheting off bare walls, thud of bare feet across bare floors, wooden flap of the kitchen screen door, rattle of dishes, splash of the shower, rock hysteria from Sage's record-player, and now and then the clatter of Sage's old car, heading down to the pass for groceries or for the laundromat.

But most often, the sounds were low decibel, for our ears only. The muffled twang of a broken coil in the mattress, the squeaky rub of sweating skins together, soft pleasure noises in the throat. Because that was what those weeks, those months, were about. We were lotus-eaters. Oh, Sage painted some. I read some. But mostly, we spent our time horizontal.

One by one, things that seemed strange and scary to me stopped being that. Even, finally, what had been scariest of all. I have read quite a bit of psychology, but I don't think they are ever going to get the answers. Why, one night, did I suddenly want it to happen—more than want, need it to happen? It didn't have anything to do with what Sage wanted. Every so often, Sage let me have signals, and I ignored them. So when it happened, it wasn't Sage who made it happen, it was me. And it wasn't like the time with Piper. No way. It was very gentle and it was good.

But afterward, things got strange. Sage kept hanging onto me. Tight. Trembling. And I felt his face wet between my shoulder blades. "What's wrong?"

He whispered, shakily, "I was scared you never would—not after what that creep did to you."

I pulled away from him and turned to face him. "It was you," I said. He sat up. I said, "You're the one who wrecked their place, smashed their music stuff. Why, Sage?"

"You walked out, remember? You weren't a faggot—especially not when I wanted you like this, in the shower. Because he'd hurt you. That was how it added up. Didn't it? You ran from me, and it was his fault."

"Ah, Christ," I said. "No, Sage."

"It wasn't any big deal to find the place," he said. "You practically drew me a map, the way you described it all. The blue cottage."

"You shouldn't have done it." I got off the bed

and went out on the balcony. I sat on the wide, flat rail with my legs hanging into the dark. I heard the small rattle of the wine jug cap. Sage came out. I said, "That equipment cost a lot of money. They needed it to earn a living."

He swung his legs over the rail, and sat with the jug between his thighs, sparks of light glittering off it, maybe from stars. "He was lucky not to be there, lucky all he lost was drums and guitars and crap. Don't worry about them. They're insured, bound to be."

"I hope so," I said.

"How did you find out about it?" He passed the jug.

"I went there looking for—something."

"It's here," he said, and took my hand and put it on his cock, that right away started to thicken.

I kissed his mouth. "Right," I said.

"I would have hacked his balls off," Sage said.

"I believe you," I said, and I did.

Because, by then, I knew about the knife. For a long while I'd seen it without knowing what I was seeing. It lay on the orange crate shelf with the matches and Zig Zag papers, crumpled dollar bills and loose change, and a dusty little drugstore alarm clock that had long ago quit ticking because there was no need for it to tick. What I saw was wooden, a shape to fit a fist, and there was a slot in it that showed a gleam of steel. A little metal knob like a rivet head was at one end of the slot. I had simply registered it. I didn't know what it

147

was. It was none of my business. Like the junk on Babe's dressing-table.

It had suddenly become my business at noon one July weekday, when it landed quivering between my naked feet with the blade sticking into the floor. Maureen had arrived, a fat girl about six feet tall, with long straight glass-color hair, and big, pink glasses. She was just back from Mexico with a cargo of new, high-quality grass, and Sage was on her list of the needy. When she pushed the door-buzzer, we were busy upstairs.

Sage seemed afraid it was his uncle or some-thing. He grabbed his pants and yanked into them and ran downstairs, zipping them. I sat there blinking for a second, then found my own pants because I was curious—we hadn't had visitors be-fore. The only people besides Sage I'd seen for a month were at the laundromat and the market. But the visit didn't last long. Just long enough for me to come down and Sage to go back up for money, and for this big, fat girl to give a bubbly laugh, call me a living doll, drape the long, loose fall of her beads over my head, drag me against her water-bed breasts, and plant a big, juicy, white lipstick kiss all over my mouth.

Then the knife went *thunk!* into the hardwood between my feet, and Maureen jumped backward with a little scream. Her beads, caught around my neck, threw me on my hands and knees, and Sage was standing over me, pushing a wad of bills at Maureen, and yanking the little pouch of clear plastic out of her hands, and telling her to get her fat, funky ass out of there, and not to try to put her blubbery cunt on me, because I was his, and if she did, he'd slice her open and pull her guts out and braid them.

She ran, he slammed the front door, came back, and pulled the knife out of the floor. He frowned at the tip, and tested it with his thumb. I guessed it was all right, because he eased the button and the blade slid back into the handle. He tossed it up and caught it and nodded to himself.

"You could have missed," I said.

He smiled and shook his head. "No."

"Don't do it again?" I said.

He started up the stairs to hide the marijuana. "Not till I have to," he said.

Two or three times we saw movies on Hollywood Boulevard. We ate out a few times at the place in the pass and out in the valley. The weather grew hot, and I asked if we couldn't go to the beach, and he didn't seem all that pleased, but we went. Venice and Santa Monica and the rest were crowded. We drove on up the coast past Zuma, and found a place you had to climb down a lot of rocks to get to. But nobody was there. We spread a blanket and lay on it. The sun baked us. We both got horny at the same minute and rolled against each other. What we did we did in a hurry and it was very basic but it felt good to do it in the middle of the day out in the open and when it was over and I got my breath back I got up and ran into the water. I swam a little way and looked back. Sage was sitting up and watching me. I shouted to him to come on in. The water was warm and felt wonderful. He got up slowly and came to the edge of the surf where it just washed shallow over his feet, but he didn't come any farther. I swam back. I waded out. I asked him to come on, but he shook his head. "I can't swim," he said.

When we got back to the canyon, signs had been posted, red and white cardboard, CONDEMNED. UNSAFE. KEEP OUT. Power had been turned off, gas, water. There was a notice in an envelope tacked to the door. It ordered us to get out. We didn't. Then a pair of young deputies arrived in a brown and white car, and stood around smoking and looking bored, while Sage and I loaded everything out of the house into Sage's car, and drove off. But we came back. After dark. Sage used a wrench to get back the water and gas. He didn't know how to manage the electricity and he was as afraid of it as he had been of the ocean. But for what we did at night we didn't need lights. We kept the refrigerator alive with chunks of ice out of a grey coin-operated machine next to the market. I didn't miss the record-player. If Sage missed it, he never said so.

One morning, he woke up with a toothache. In a new tooth, a wisdom tooth, way at the back. When there was daylight enough for me to see it, it looked bad, a bluish black color. Sage's October check from his foster father was overdue. We had about two dollars and change, not enough for a dentist. Sage sent me down to the pass for whiskey. What you do, he said, is take a mouthful of whiskey and hold it. It numbs the nerve. Naturally, swallowing the whiskey helps too. I left him suffering. I can't drive, so I walked down to the market. Mr. Myers, at the liquor counter, said I was too young, but he knew Sage wasn't from the I.D. Sage showed him when he cashed his checks, and when I explained the whiskey was for Sage and why, he let me take half a pint. Everyone who worked in that market knew us.

When I got back, I heard talking upstairs. Why it scared me, I didn't know, but it did. Maybe I thought the way we'd been living was too good to last. The years with Babe had taught me to take cover when things started running too smoothly. So I climbed the stairs, cautious and quiet in my rubber soles. At the landing halfway up, I could make out words, and I stopped. I didn't know the voice.

"When I got back to Hollywood," it said, "the word was around that he was dead."

"You didn't see it," Sage said. "You split."

"You bet your ass I split. Clear back home to Texas. You knifed him. Why wouldn't I be next?"

"I didn't knife him," Sage said.

"You sure as hell had that knife in your hand. You sure as hell cut at him. If you didn't slice him up, it was only because he jumped first."

"I wasn't even gay," Sage said. "I only did it with him because he kept after me, saying he loved me, he'd kill himself if I wouldn't. He didn't want to live if he couldn't have me. Shit! Then I come up here and find him in the sack with you! How would you take it, for Christ sake?"

151

"Pay me." The voice was bored. "Just pay me."

Coins rattled on the floor. "That's all I've got."

"You got a check. Yesterday. You get one the fifteenth of every month. I've seen you cash it at the market. Since I heard he died, since I heard the police think it was murder only they don't know who, I've been watching you. Who sends the checks? Who are you blackmailing?"

"Nobody," Sage said. "And the check hasn't come."

"When it does, it's mine, or I go to the police."

"Get lost," Sage said.

I ran up the rest of the stairs and smashed the bottle against the doorframe. They turned and looked at me. The hustler was Sage's age and coloring but smaller. He had a little copper color pistol in his hand, but he'd forgotten it. Which was all the chance Sage needed. He grabbed his knife. Its blade flicked out like a tin snake's tongue and drew a red line across the fingers on the gun butt. The hustler's eyes opened wide, and he dropped the gun, and Sage kicked it under the bed. He started to throw me a smile, but it didn't last.

I lunged at him, raking with the neck of the broken bottle at his face. Not fast enough. He caught my wrist and I was off my feet and turning over in the air. I hit the far edge of the bed, and spilled off it onto the floor. The French doors were open back of me, and Sage was coming at me with the knife. The hustler had gone. Getting up, I dragged the blanket off the bed and looped it at the hand that held the knife, but I missed. And Sage came on. I backed and was on the balcony, and there was nowhere to go to get away from him except out and down.

And that was where I went.

now it's two in the morning, and I am lying among Taco Bell boxes and paperback books in the raunchy bed in the old house on the beach, and blinking up half blinded by the ceiling light at Catch and Lieutenant Sewell. Catch looks like a corpse—one that's died of fright. He's in his green hospital outfit, and his hands are in back of him, and he is crying.

"I couldn't help it," he says.

"Hello, Alan," Sewell says. "How are you?"

"Eight hours of sleep per night," I say, "are essential to the health of growing boys and girls. Especially is this true during adolescence, when important changes are taking place in the—"

"You're all right." Sewell sounds relieved.

"I told you he was all right," Catch says. "Now, will you take these handcuffs off me?"

"I don't think the taxpayers will mind if I let you wear them a little longer."

"He can't sit up unless I help him," Catch says. I have let him go on believing that. It reinforces his ego, the motherhood component.

"I'll help him," Sewell says. He takes me under the arms, and I do nothing to make it easier for him. Dragging me upright, Sewell grunts and sweat breaks out on his forehead. The casts are heavy. My back is against a wall that is hard and cold with sea damp.

"Can I have my pillows?" I say.

Sewell locates them on the floor on the other side of the bed, and shoves them behind me. Not gently. He says, "You want to take off your sweatshirt?"

"Not especially," I say.

"Take it off anyway," he says.

"I'm susceptible to colds," I say.

"Alan, your friend Jackson here is in trouble."

I look at Catch, and Catch looks back at me like a man in trouble, and I pull the sweatshirt off over my head. Sewell blinks at the new bandages. Then he grips my shoulder, hinges me forward, finds the tape, yanks that off, and unwinds the gauze, with motions like lasso spinning. He bends and squints at my scars, nods, straightens up. He lets the gauze snake out of his hand onto the bed with the ashtray and the greasy burrito wrappers.

"Now, will you fold back the blankets, please?"

I pretend to be Catch's imaginary mother. I look indignant. "Now you jus' see heah," I say, "ah may be only a sick ol' lady, but ah still has mah dignity. Mistah po-leesmans, suh, please—I ain' got no pants on." I want Catch to laugh or even smile, or at least stop his silent crying. But he doesn't.

"Show him the casts," he says.

"What do they want to do to you?" I ask him.

"Prove that I stabbed you, kidnapped you."

I look at Sewell with what I hope is contempt. Also incredulity. Contemptuous incredulity. "After those idiots at that hospital put me in that little

154

room when they were through doping me and setting my legs, and after some son of a bitch came in the dark and stuck a knife in me half a dozen times, I felt a little insecure, Lieutenant. The nurses had all run off to look at a fire in a closet on some other corridor. Doctors too, if any. Catch was the only person around. I asked him please to get me out of there."

"Can I see the casts, please?"

I throw back the covers. Sewell looks and nods and sighs. "Okay." He bends and drags the covers over me again, then sits on the bed and studies me. "You *asked* Jackson to get you out?"

"I told you," Catch says.

"Shut up, Jackson, please." Sewell doesn't look at Catch. He looks at me. "Because some unknown assailant tried to kill you?" He shakes his head. "I can see the knife wounds, so I believe that. What I don't believe was that the assailant was unknown. I think you knew damn good and well who it was."

I feel cold in the pit of my stomach. "No."

"It was the same person who, a few hours before, tried to kill you by pushing you, or throwing you, off the balcony of what had been your father's apartment—in a building that has since been condemned and abandoned. Since his death, I mean."

I looked wide-eyed. "Why would anyone do that to me?"

"Because you found out they killed your father."

"Aren't you forgetting," I said. "My father dived for some blowing papers and lost his balance. Accident."

Sewell ignores that. "But you were luckier than he was. You only broke your legs. And you didn't bleed to death, in spite of the fact the fractures were compound and the bone splinters were sticking through the flesh, and you didn't die of shock and exposure, because two water department engineers checking some surveying errors up in that canyon happened to stumble across you."

"I don't remember much about that," I say, and it's the truth. "How did you get to Catch? Jackson, I mean? Where did that picture come from you're showing around?"

"I got to Jackson through a coverall like the one he's wearing now. The hospital laundry records showed one missing for the shift when you disappeared from the hospital. Jackson wasn't able to give a coherent story as to why he hadn't turned his coverall in. I thought maybe it was bloodstained—with your blood. The bed was soaked, wasn't it? Checking laundry records isn't exactly inspired police work, but in this case it paid off."

"What paid off was, he put the arm on me for murder," Catch says. "And I didn't know what kind of mess you in, but it wasn't nothing you done. You told me that. Nothing you done. Didn't you tell me that?"

I nod and try to smile—Catch looks so miserable. He manages a wobbly smile. I say to Sewell, "I never told anyone my name—not in the ambulance, not at the hospital. Did I? Was I delirious?"

"You were in shock. You didn't open your mouth. The hospital, reasonably enough, listed you as another runaway juvenile. Los Angeles gets more than its share."

"As a matter of fact, I'm thirty-six years old."

"Sure you are." Sewell's smile is thin. "They also assumed you'd been exploring those condemned buildings at the head of the canyon, and had fallen."

I shake my head. "No. I'm crazy about pinyon nuts. I climbed a pine tree after pinyon nuts, and in my trembling eagerness, I slipped and fell. You still haven't told me how you found out about it."

"I had occasion to be checking juvenile files day before yesterday, trying to get a line on a boy found dead and naked in a trash bag, and I ran across your description. It couldn't have been anybody else. And with it was the address where the ambulance had picked you up, an address I remembered, your father's address. I didn't like the coincidence, and I drove over to the hospital for a word with you.

"And I learned about the bloody bed with nobody in it. The investigating officer from the precinct where the hospital is located didn't do too well with that. His wife was sick at the time, and one of his own kids had taken off for parts unknown." Sewell opens his jacket to get to an inside pocket, and I see a little gun butt sticking out of a holster under his arm. "I had a police artist draw you from my description." He hands me an oblong of paper.

I unfold it and look at it and pass it back to him. "The eyes are too close together," I say.

He shrugs. "They knew you." He folds the paper and puts it away, showing the gun again. "So— I went back to work, found out about the fire in the closet, about everything that happened on that shift, more than I wanted to know, but also what I needed to know. First the missing orderly's overall, then the fact that not only did Jackson, here, not run to the fire with everyone else, but no one could remember seeing him the rest of that night. A gurney with bloodsoaked sheets was found abandoned in the employee's parking lot. I had a look inside Jackson's car and found a lot of dried blood. Naturally, I found Jackson. I didn't think I'd find you. Not alive."

"He's all right," Catch says. "I been looking after him."

"Did you do the doctoring too?" Sewell asks. "Those wounds were stitched. And very professionally. You practice medicine without a license, Jackson?"

"I did it myself," I tell him. "I keep a sewing kit handy at all times. In case I get a run in my nylons. You get lots of runs climbing trees."

"If this is how you act at home," Sewell says, "you didn't run away—your mother threw you out." He looks around disgustedly at the room. "What do you want to stay in a place like this for?"

"Catch and I are in love," I say. "We're going to be married." And I nearly crack up at how this jolts Catch, who doesn't know whether to stand there scared to death, or run out and order the invitations.

Sewell stands up. "Tell me who tried to kill you. They murdered your father. Why protect them?"

I push down in the bed and drag the covers over my face. "I'm tired," I say.

Sewell jerks the covers off me. "Listen to me. I

can take you to Juvenile Hall right now, and stick you there until you're ready to cooperate."

"I was knifed by a doctor with a Transylvanian accent. He's constructing a superman. He wanted my brain. It's a terrific brain. It goes right off the top of the IQ charts. Look him up at the hospital. Name starts with an F." I wrinkle my childish brow in concentration. I snap my fingers and smile. "I've got it—Frankenstein."

"Okay." Sewell tramps to the door and shouts into the hall. "Taylor! Help me get him out to the car."

"If you put me in Juvenile Hall," I say, "it'll be just like the hospital. Except this time he won't miss. This time, he'll kill me."

"Not if you tell me who he is," Sewell says.

I sit up and shout at him. "You're the genius detective. You find out who he is. In case you don't remember—I tried to help you when my father was killed. You were too God damn smart to listen." The weary man from Sewell's office stands by him now in the doorway. I yell at them both. "I'm safe here. Nobody knows I'm here. Nobody but you. If you'd just forgotten about me, the way you forgot about my father—"

"Hold it." Sewell doesn't say it loudly, but he means it, and I drop back on the pillows. Sewell scowls at me. Not at me—through me. He reaches under his jacket to scratch. He takes a breath. "All right. I'll leave you here. And you'll stay here, too, because before I drive away from here tonight, there'll be a man from the Department standing outside watching this place. And when he goes home, another man will replace him. Around the clock.

"And tomorrow morning, I'm going to start asking questions. About your father's death. And everyone I ask, is going to be told where you are. And one of them is going to come here. You know which one. And when he does, we'll have him, won't we? Of course you could save us a lot of trouble and time and money. You could just give me his name."

"I want my sweatshirt," I say, "I'm cold."

"Come on, Taylor," Sewell says. "Let's go."

"The handcuffs!" Catch yelps.

Sewell takes them off him. He looks disgustedly at me, but he keeps his mouth shut. He and Taylor go heavily down the stairs. Catch rubs his wrists. Then he comes to the bed and puts my sweatshirt on me.

It rains hard. The wind forgets and remembers. When it remembers, it throws the rain against the window like gravel. It shakes the house. Catch stands in the door of my room. Through his transparent plastic raincoat, I see that he is dressed up. He doesn't have to tell me what for. He's going to look for a job. He sets a mug of fresh coffee down at Kwan Yin's feet.

"Don't go," I say. "The cop isn't out there."

"He probably sitting in his car out back. Anyway, nobody going to come here in weather like this. Not for any reason. He know that. You know that. I know that. It why I'm going today, not yesterday."

"Get Doc, then. Please."

"Doc up at the Work Farm. Thirty days." Catch bends and kisses me. "We got to have bread, baby." He smiles and strokes my hair. "You lose any more weight, and I won't be able to see you for looking."

"If he kills me, you won't. For sure."

"You paranoid," he says. "Listen to that storm."

He goes, and I listen to it. And he doesn't come back. An hour goes on for two. Two will get you four. I watch the mirror. The beach is empty. No sign of the officer supposed to be protecting me. I try the radio for Bach. I try to read. And a window breaks—a downstairs window at the rear. So the watch cop isn't out back in his car. I never thought he was. You know when you're alone. And the steps come, long-legged, up the stairs, two at a time. And Sage is standing in the doorway. He's wet. All he's worn is a blue workshirt with the tails out, and thin jeans. And his car has no roof, and the drive is miles and miles. He's soaked. We stare at each other. Finally, I say:

"Where's the knife?"

He pats his gut. "Here." He comes three steps into the room.

"Don't wait," I tell him. "Do it. Only don't mess up this time." I pull the sweatshirt up and put a fingertip on my chest. "The heart is here."

Sage shakes his head. "No. I only tried it because I thought you were going to tell the police."

"Why did you wait till I was in the hospital? I was down there under the trees for hours. My parachute didn't open."

"You're still funny." His smile is sad. "I figured

you were dead. Like Eric. I went to find the hustler."

"And did you find him?"

Sage nods. "Carved E on one side of his ass and T on the other. He said he wouldn't talk, and he hasn't. When I got back, the ambulance was there, and I heard you scream. It shook me. I followed it. Man, that hospital was full of people."

"You knew how to handle that," I say. "You set fire to a janitor's closet."

"Only the spade didn't go," he says.

"He thought maybe he could do something for me to make me forget the pain. And he has."

Sage ignores that. "Why didn't you cop out?"

"It was my father you killed. It was me you lied to. It was my body you used. Who owed it to kill you? Some civil servant who doesn't even know you?"

"You?" Sage smiles, very skeptical.

"When these casts came off. I hate you, Sage."

It goes like a slap across his face. "Eric was a shit. You know he was a shit. All those friends of his told you what a shit he was. How can you hate *me*?"

"If you don't know, I can't explain."

But he knows. Face wooden, he comes to the bed, digs the knife from his waistband, and touches the button so the blade jumps out. He turns the knife and hands it to me, handle first. He peels off the wet shirt, unbuckles his belt and his wet pants fall. He is barefoot, and he steps out of the pants and gets on the bed and straddles me. He taps his own chest.

"There," he says. "Make your fist tight. And hit as hard as you can."

I stare at the place, smooth and brown. I can see the heart bump, like an unborn child trying to get out. I close my hand tight around the handle of the knife and raise my arm. Sage doesn't move. He is looking down at my face, and I can feel the look, and I don't want to look at his face, but I can't help myself. I don't know what is in his eyes. The window light is grey from the rain and the grey clouds his eyes.

"Do it," he says. "Do it now."

But I can't make my arm move. I can't kill the child in there. I shake my head and drop the knife. And Sage is kissing me, lying on me heavy, the way he used to. His tongue wants into my mouth, and I let it in. I just let it in. It doesn't mean anything. Less than food. He stops trying that, and tries other things, every loving thing he knows, things I'm long familiar with, things that used to be very good. They're no good now.

I lie propped against the pillows and watch him, with his long, rainsoaked hair, trying, trying hard and getting nowhere, nowhere. It isn't disgusting, not even pathetic. It's nothing. And at last he looks up at me, and he's crying. And he does what I know he is going to do. It's not easy, but he's strong. He flops me onto my face. I don't even jerk from the first hurt. I just lie there and let it happen. When it's over, he collapses on my back, sobbing. I say nothing because there is nothing to say.

"Love me?" he pleads. "Love me, Alan?"

But he knows better, and finally gets up, and there are sounds that say he's dressing. I push away the pillows so I can see his beautiful nakedness vanish into the wet pants, the wet shirt. I expect it to make me sad, because I know I'm seeing it for the last time. But it doesn't make me sad. It doesn't make me feel. Anything. The shirt is buttoned, and he looks at me, begging with his eyes, and I turn my face away, turn my face to the wall.

I don't hear motion. I don't know what he is doing. Probably just staring at me. He used to like to do that. He would spend thoughtful time hunting up words to describe me to myself. He used to snap pencils after trying to draw me for hours and not getting it right. The drawings looked good to me, but he always ripped them up, disgusted.

I ask the wall, "Whose initials are you going to carve on my ass?"

There's no answer. I turn my head again. He is gone. I grab the edge of the mattress and drag myself around so that by half breaking my neck, I can see up into the mirror. There's still no sign of the watch cop on the beach. No one is on the beach. The rain and wind punish the dark sand. The surf hits it like falling tombstones. The pier is empty. A long streamer of rag knotted around the railing lashes in the wind. A big naked tincan rolls along the grey cement. Then the pier isn't empty. Sage walks out on it, slowly, head lowered, butting the wind, walks straight out on it, walks right up the middle, shirt tails flapping when the wind catches them, flapping heavy with rain.

And I feel. Suddenly I feel. "No," I say, and I struggle to get myself, the top half, off the bed and, gripping the bed leg, try to drag the casts after me. I grope back to try to lift them, lose my balance, twist, and land on the back of my neck. And the casts crash down. I sit up and lift the left one over the right, and let its weight flop me onto my belly. Then I crawl for the window, clawing the gritty rug, dragging the casts. And it takes too much time. When I get there, and grab the sill to pull myself up, Sage is small and rain-blurred at the far end of the pier. I break into a sweat, trying to hold myself up with one hand while I push at the window with the other. I break a thumbnail. I try again, and the window shudders up, and rain blows on my face.

I shout, "No, Sage! No!"

But it's too far, and the storm is too loud. He can't hear. Anything. He climbs over the steel rail at the circular end of the pier. He holds the rail for a moment. Then he drops. And I have to let go of the window sill because I can't hold on any longer. I half curl against the wall under the window, and the rain falls in on me, and I chill, and can't stop shivering. The rain runs down the wall, soaking the old paper, turning it browner than time has already turned it.

I take a breath, and hoist myself by my fingers again, and with my chin on the sill, I try to see through the rain. Nothing. I let myself down again and rest again. And the next time I look out, Sage is lying on the sand, with the surf rolling him, and the shirt washed up over his face. And the dogs are nosing him. Those dogs sure as hell don't care about the weather.

"I'm watching you!" I shout. "I'm watching you!"

They can't hear, of course, but they back off. One of them turns, suddenly, and starts to savage another one. Then they all stiffen, looking in the same direction. Then they run, because the cop who was supposed to be standing out there in the storm watching the house comes pounding heavily along the soaked sand, holding his canvas rain hat by the brim to keep it from blowing off. And another man comes running behind him. They both crouch over Sage, and the second man's hat blows off, and I see that he is Sewell. He gets to his feet and drags Sage up away from the wash of the surf. He straddles Sage and tries to pump the water out of him. He looks back toward the house. I doubt that I can be seen, but I drop anyway.

They must both be working on Sage because no one comes. Not for a long time. I lie curled up with the rain falling on me. I get waves of shuddering from the cold. I sneeze and sneeze. Then Sewell comes in. He calls my name and stops dead for a minute because I am not in the bed. Then I sneeze again and he sees me under the window. He runs to me, falls to his knees. "Are you all right?" He starts to touch me and is afraid to.

"I'm going to have a terrible cold," I say.

"Dear God," he says, and picks me up and puts me on the bed. He slams down the window, goes out and down the hall, and brings a towel from the bathroom. He dries me with it, roughly, hurriedly. He jerks the covers over me and paws in the rubble on the bed for the sweatshirt. He yanks this over my head, and tries to help me with the arms but I do it myself. Sewell gives me the towel and I dry my hair with it.

"You lived with him all summer," Sewell says. "In your father's old apartment. No—he didn't tell me. He told me he'd only seen you once, the day after I saw you. But I showed your picture at the local supermarket. They told me different. I went back to find him. Place was empty. His car was gone. I thought he'd be coming here. But the freeway was a mess because of the rain. I kept getting jammed up, couldn't make any time." He studies my face. I can't seem to stop tears from running down it. He says, "He was the one who killed your father—right?"

"Is he all right?" I say. "Did you save him?"

"He's dead," Sewell says.

"He was the one who killed my father," I say because it doesn't matter now. "Look, will you see if you can find Catch for me? I'd like to have Catch come home."